I'm not convinced

About the Author

BETH GOOBIE studied literature and creative writing at the universities of Winnipeg and Alberta. Her stories have appeared in magazines such as the *Capilano Review, Event, Grain* and *Fiddlehead,* and her previous books include *Who Owns Kelly Paddik?, Could I have My Body Back Now, Please?,* and *Mission Impossible,* which earned her a Governor General's Award nomination for Children's Literature.

"[Goobie] demonstrates talent and understanding; above all, she creates a voice that speaks to modern teens. It's a voice that deserves to be heard." (from a starred review of *Mission Impossible* in *Quill & Quire)*

I'm not convinced

Beth Goobie

NORTHERN LIGHTS YOUNG NOVELS

Red Deer College Press

Northern Lights Young Novels are published by
Red Deer College Press
56 Avenue & 32 Street Box 5005
Red Deer Alberta Canada T4N 5H5

Credits
Edited for the Press by Tim Wynne Jones and Peter Carver.
Cover art and design by Jeff Hitch.
Text design by Dennis Johnson.
Printed and bound in Canada by Webcom Limited for
Red Deer College Press.

Acknowledgments
Financial support provided by the Alberta Foundation for the
Arts, a beneficiary of the Lottery Fund of the Government of
Alberta, and by the Canada Council, the Department of Canadi-
an Heritage and Red Deer College.

THE CANADA COUNCIL | LE CONSEIL DES ARTS
FOR THE ARTS | DU CANADA
SINCE 1957 | DEPUIS 1957

COMMITTED TO THE DEVELOPMENT OF CULTURE AND THE ARTS

Canadian Cataloguing in Publication Data
Goobie, Beth, 1959–
I'm not convinced
(Northern lights young novels)
ISBN 0-88995-159-4
I. Title II. Series
PS8563.O8326I5 1997   jC813'.54   C96-910775-7
PZ7.G6331m 1997

6   5   4   3   2   1

The author thanks the following people for their contributions to the manuscript: Mrs. Sands, Tatjana Stenferd-Kroese, Karen Alliston, Lorne Cardinal, Peter Carver and Tim Wynne-Jones.

for Pam

I'm Not Convinced

Chapter 1

Sharon Frejer had no face. At least, that was the way it felt. Sometime before kindergarten, it must've gone underground because all her school photographs showed only a shirt buttoned up to her chin and a clump of brown hair.

"The only way I can tell your front from your back is by your buttons," her mother would complain.

Sharon used her hair as camouflage. She thought of it as a good place to hide out, kind of like the Vietnam jungle. The main problem was that in order to make her shoulder-length hair slide across her face, she had to look down. It meant she spent most of her time observing the world that went on below her nose—bugs, puddles, people's feet.

It was eyes that Sharon Frejer wanted to avoid. She knew that if eyes got past the thick, brown clump of hair that she wore over her face, they'd see she was weird, she was ugly. Sharon Frejer just wanted to be ignored as much as possible.

About a month ago, Sharon and her mother had moved to Edmonton to live with her Uncle Bert. Everything—the sidewalks, the houses, even the sky—still felt new. On top of this, today was her first day of grade eight in a new school, where everyone else already knew each other. With her head angled to the side so she could see through cracks in her hair, Sharon studied the schedule she'd been given in home room. Her next subject was Home Economics. Ahead of her, the class of chattering voices and feet turned right, into a doorway. Shrinking down between her shoulders, she shuffled quickly into the room and looked around for the nearest empty desk.

Several long tables stretched out. There was an unoccupied chair at the end of a nearby table. Quickly, Sharon scuffed over to it and plunked herself down.

"Good morning, class. I'm Ms. Bohn," said a voice.

Through her hair, Sharon could see the lower half of a very thin woman stalking around between the tables, bouncing a meter stick against one palm. She was listing off the rules that applied to the Home Ec. classroom. She pronounced *rules* as *rools.*

"We will begin with the General Classroom Rools," Ms. Bohn announced.

Panic flew through Sharon like a sudden flock of birds. Her Uncle Bert, who also traded *u*'s for *oo*'s, had stepped into her head. "Stoopid!" he yelled. "You're stoopid!"

Uncle Bert spent a lot of time yelling in Sharon's head. "Stoopid!" he'd boom, and the *oo*'s would echo, getting louder and rounder between her ears. Staring down, her hair falling forward, Sharon would feel as if her face were beginning to melt. Then the Black Hole would show up in her brain and suck her face in. The room would go black. Sounds would disappear. It'd be impossible to breathe. After a while, when things were all right again, her face would come back so she could feel it where it was supposed to be. None of her health or science teachers had ever mentioned the possibility of disappearing body parts, but this Black Hole bit had been happening to Sharon for as long as she could remember. It was her reason for the kamikaze hairstyle, and she kept it a personal secret.

Sharon could hear Uncle Bert at it now in her head, telling her how stoopid she'd be at sewing, cooking, even at wiping a counter clean. Behind Uncle Bert's voice, Ms. Bohn was still going on about her rules. Sharon could see it coming. She'd forget the most important rule. Ms. Bohn would notice. She'd yell at her in front of the entire class.

Then, just above Sharon's head, Ms. Bohn's voice stopped and began to discuss sewing machines. A finger descended onto Sharon's right shoulder. "I'd like your assistance with this demonstration," the voice said.

Sharon wanted to say, "I can't—I'm too stoopid." She shrank down into her seat.

"What's your name?"

"Sharon." There—she'd managed to say something. This was a positive sign. Keeping her head down, Sharon pushed back her chair and followed Ms. Bohn's shiny black marching shoes around the tables. Sharon had sub-zero knowledge about sewing machines. She was certain that if she touched one of those intricate, technological operations with her stoopid hands, it'd explode.

Sharon lowered herself into the chair in front of the sewing machine. Ms. Bohn's voice went on and on about this and that regarding sewing machines, and Sharon's sweating hands tried to do what they were supposed to do. Peering through the cracks in her hair, she seemed to be managing. Ms. Bohn was almost at the end of her demonstration when Sharon realized, surprised, that she was still alive. Nothing had blown up. The end of the world hadn't happened. Perhaps someone new had taken over the universe and things would improve.

"Please put the machine away."

It was over. Sharon took hold of the machine and lowered it into its cupboard. Almost down—in two seconds everyone would peel their eyes off her. Then the machine slipped. It slipped out of her sweaty hands and thudded into the bottom of its case.

"What was that?!" Ms. Bohn snapped.

Sharon ducked farther in behind her hair. The universe was back to its usual state of affairs.

"This was an error, class. This was an error that could severely damage a machine. Whoever damages a machine out of carelessness like this will pay the costs of repair."

"Idiot!" boomed Uncle Bert.

The Black Hole bit was happening. Sharon's face began to melt.

"Take the machine out again if you think you can manage," said Ms. Bohn.

Sharon had the feeling Ms. Bohn wasn't really offering her an option. She wiped her sweating hands on her pants and tried to keep her arms steady. Any second now, she knew, the machine would roll out of her hands like a well-aimed bowling ball.

"Excuse me, Ms. Bohn?"

Ready to start lifting, Sharon froze. Here she was on Death Row. Who was crazy enough to open her mouth at a time like this?

"Yes?" Ms. Bohn turned toward the new voice.

"I'd like to help." Sharon heard the girl stand up, then walk across the room. "We have a sewing machine at home. I use it all the time. Sometimes ours gets really slippery."

Sharon stood, careful not to move. What would Ms.

Bohn do about this girl just up and walking around? There must be some rule about not getting up and going for a walk around the room without permission.

"What's your name?"

"Fern Thompson."

"Go ahead, then."

Two hands appeared opposite Sharon's. Between the four hands, the machine rose smoothly into an upright position. Ms. Bohn swooped forward, poking at every knob and button, muttering under her breath. Sharon noticed the girl beside her was wearing black rubber boots with orange toes and heels. It was a hot, sunny day outside.

Ms. Bohn straightened. "You must be an exceptionally fortunate young lady, Sharon. Everything seems to be in order. Now, we'll watch you put it back in properly."

The machine felt as if it was the size and weight of a refrigerator, but the four hands lowered it easily into the cupboard. This Fern girl had saved her life, Sharon thought. She also realized, suddenly, that above everything in the entire world, she hated sewing machines.

"That is sufficient," Ms. Bohn said.

Back in her seat, Sharon shot a few quick glances in the direction of Fern Thompson. The girl had a mass of blonde, curly hair that belonged in a shampoo ad. As Sharon watched, the girl's mouth made slow, secretive chewing motions around an illegal gum wad. Sharon slid farther down into her chair and hung extra hair over her face.

Ms. Bohn began to discuss the Wash-Up Rules.

Chapter 2

Later that day, Sharon's Language Arts teacher, Ms. Okashimo, smiled and picked up a piece of paper from her desk. Sharon wondered if they were about to hear the L.A. classroom rules, but Ms. Okashimo requested they write down their hobbies, then sent the list down the first row.

As she waited for the list, Sharon studied her desk top. Hobbies—she didn't have a lot of hobbies. Mostly, she read books, four to six a week during the summer. When she got tired of reading, she played with paper dolls.

Sharon knew this was not normal. Playing with paper dolls was certainly not something to write down on a class hobby list, but what else was she supposed to do with her time? If she watched TV, she had to sit next to Uncle Bert and watch hockey. She didn't have brothers or sisters, and she'd never been good at making friends. Other kids seemed so different. They were always dashing off toward the horizon, shouting and laughing as they moved on to whatever it was they had to do. Sharon couldn't remember a time when she had something to look forward to.

When the list slid onto her desk, Sharon tilted her head to one side and scanned it. She couldn't leave it blank, but she didn't want to lie, either. In the end, she decided to write with her left hand. Ms. Okashimo was sure to ignore sloppy handwriting. Sharon passed the list on.

As Ms. Okashimo read the list a few minutes later, Sharon began to get a very bad feeling about grade eight.

"There are some pretty interesting hobbies listed here," said Ms. Okashimo. "I think this would be a good way to get to know each other. I'd like a few of you to talk to the rest of the class about your hobbies. I see a Len Razlaff wrote down scuba diving. Who is Len Razlaff?"

Ms. Okashimo tossed her gaze across the class. Over by the window, a boy with an earring shifted, then raised his hand. If he hadn't had an earring, Sharon might've felt sorry for him, but she figured boys with earrings were tough enough to handle anything. Scuba diving, she thought admiringly.

Ms. Okashimo checked Len Razlaff off for a presentation. As she refocused on her list, an enormous smile dragged itself across her face.

It's coming, Sharon thought.

"And I see we have a very unusual hobby here. Sharon Frejer?"

Someone had buttoned up Sharon's voice.

"Sharon Frejer?" repeated Ms. Okashimo.

Sharon shoved her right hand into the air.

"Such an unusual hobby." Ms. Okashimo's smile was very encouraging. "Paper dolls."

Snickers broke out across the class. Ms. Okashimo ditched her smile and pulled out a frown. "D'you collect special paper dolls, Sharon?"

"I'm not sure." Sharon had the feeling her paper dolls were far from special. Most of them came from Zellers.

"Well, why don't you bring in a few and tell us about

them?" ordered Ms. Okashimo, making another giant
check mark on her list. "Coral Sanderson?"

Sharon pretended the hair she'd dumped across her
face meant she couldn't see the other kids turning in
their seats to look back at her. That blonde girl, Fern, was
watching her again. Sharon became suddenly very busy
examining the top of her desk for pen marks. Heat
stained her face.

"Coral Sanderson is learning to pilot an airplane?"
Ms. Okashimo asked.

Sharon realized her presentation about paper dolls
would be sandwiched between one about scuba diving
and one about piloting an airplane. Tears bloomed in her
eyes. Inside her head, Uncle Bert got going.

"You're real stoopid, Sharon. I can hardly believe how
stoopid you are," he roared. It was difficult to sniff without making any noise. Sharon found some of the toilet
paper she'd folded up to look like Kleenex in her pencil
case and tried to blow her nose daintily. She sounded like
a dainty vacuum cleaner.

Either her entire brain had just turned into one giant
tumor, or her whole purpose in coming to Edmonton
and a new junior high school was to continue as a huge
social failure. And spell that, she thought, in capital letters.

Chapter 3

Whenever Sharon walked up to the house on 124th Street, she thought of it as Uncle Bert's house. It was old. Its two storeys were built over and behind Uncle Bert's grocery store. The store was open until 6:00 P.M., which meant Uncle Bert was out of Sharon's life until supper-time.

Still, the place never stopped feeling like Uncle Bert's house. Uncle Bert allowed only forty-watt bulbs. Most of the shades were pulled down, and every room smelled like a basement. Uncle Bert thought of everything as a price. He thought of the cereal Sharon ate in the morning as a dollar he could've made in the store. She understood that the milk she poured into the bowl cost him fifty cents and that two spoonfuls of sugar were worth ten cents. Sharon figured her Uncle Bert probably thought she was born with TWENTY-FIVE DOLLARS A DAY stamped on her forehead.

That summer, Sharon and her mother had taken the bus across the prairies from Rockwood, Ontario, to Edmonton, Alberta. They were moving across three provinces, Sharon had thought. That was far enough to make big changes. She'd stared out the bus window as they'd passed through Thunder Bay, Winnipeg, Regina and Calgary, through fields of canola, grain, and corn. Finally, in the distance, she'd seen the Rocky Mountains, gray-blue and unreal against the sky like cardboard cutouts.

During the bus ride, Sharon's mother had worn a small smile. She'd even laughed a few times. After arriving in Edmonton, it'd only taken about a day and a half for her mother to change back to the person she'd been in Rockwood. All the lines showed up on her face again.

The smile crawled back somewhere inside her mouth. Since they'd arrived, Sharon's mother had swept the floors, cooked the meals, and helped in the store. If she had the time, she sat, watched TV, and smoked. When she tucked Sharon in at night, she asked, "How was your day?"

Sharon always replied, "Fine."

Tonight, as her mother stood by the stove, ladling out stew, Sharon set her retainer next to her plate and bowed her head. Uncle Bert said grace. Then Sharon waited for her mother to dish out the food. It wasn't an overly intelligent idea to talk around Uncle Bert, especially when he was hungry. Sometimes breathing was inadvisable.

"You look like a dog."

Sharon didn't argue the point. She could feel the Black Hole getting into gear and let her hair fall farther forward.

"Don't we got any rubber bands? Hey, Caroline—don't we got any rubber bands in this house? I mean, you ain't no beauty, kid, but a face is better-looking than a dog's hind end."

"Here's your supper, Bert," her mother said anxiously. "Want me to work on the filing later?"

"Yeah—the invoices need straightening out." Once he had his food, Uncle Bert usually left everyone else alone.

"How's school going?" her mother asked.

Sharon poked at a potato. "Okay. This girl helped me in Home Ec. a couple of days ago."

"She know what your face looks like?" muttered Uncle Bert.

The potato fell apart. "Her name's Fern."

"With a name like that, she's probably got a fag for a father."

"I dunno," said Sharon. She pushed her carrots around between chunks of meat and potato.

"What're the other kids like?" asked her mother.

"Okay, I guess. They do things like scuba diving. There's a girl who pilots an airplane."

Uncle Bert snorted. "Some dame came up to me in the store today, wanted . . ." Most of the people Uncle Bert met seemed to be stupider than the average knucklehead. Uncle Bert went on about general stupidity until he shoved his chair back and left the table.

For a moment, Sharon's mother sat in exactly the same position, as if bracing herself against her brother's return. Then she ran a hand across her forehead, brushing away a small wisp of brown hair. "Everything is going to be just fine," she whispered to herself.

Sharon felt a rush of pain. Her mother was hurting again. She stood and circled her arms around her mother's neck. "I'm okay, Mom. Don't worry about me."

"Maybe if you just asked him how he was—how his day went?" suggested her mother. "Bert's a fine man. He cares about you. He just doesn't know how to communicate."

Sharon knew her mother was afraid Uncle Bert would kick them out, like her Uncle Lawrence had in Rockwood. Her mother had dropped out of high school and had a difficult time looking for jobs.

"Just try a little harder with your uncle, okay Sharon?" her mother asked.

Sharon hugged her mother closer. She'd try anything for her. "Okay, Mom, I'll try. I promise."

Chapter 4

On Friday afternoon, Sharon pushed herself up from her desk into a great silence. She picked up the envelope on her desk and meandered to the front of the classroom, taking note of every type of shoe that stuck out into the aisle. That Fern girl was wearing rubber boots again.

Ms. Okashimo had moved from the front of the classroom to the side window so that Sharon would have more room to herself. An empty space, large enough to contain several galaxies, had moved into Sharon's brain. She stood staring down at the blue-green linoleum. Kids began to shift and giggle in their desks.

"Why don't you show us some of your paper dolls?" prompted Ms. Okashimo.

Sharon wasn't sure her hands were working properly. She tried holding the envelope with one hand and reaching into it with the other. The hand came out with the cardboard figure of Barbie. She held the hand and the paper doll up in the air.

"Here's one of them," she mumbled. She put it down on Ms. Okashimo's desk. Some of the boys snorted. Sharon pulled out another.

"Here's another one," she said.

Why had Ms. Okashimo thought this would be interesting? Sharon reached in and pulled out another figure. "Here's another one." After this, her arm went automatic. Her brain shut down and the arm pulled out figure after figure, waved them around in the air, then placed them onto the desk beside her.

She could hear kids starting to laugh. Someone muttered, "Oh, brother."

Sharon wasn't sure how long Ms. Okashimo wanted her to stand there, waving paper dolls in the air. Now the kids were hooting. Ms. Okashimo tried to shush them, but laughter rolled out of their mouths, filling the aisles. Sharon kept pulling out more paper dolls, waving them in the air, then depositing them on the desk until the envelope was empty. Then she stood, holding the empty envelope and staring at the blue-green linoleum. The laughter swirled up in small snorts and gurgles around the room. Sharon waited for Ms. Okashimo to tell her what to do next.

There was a pause from the window. The teacher cleared her throat. "Well, Sharon . . ." she began.

The laughter broke out again, but this time Ms. Okashimo yelled and the kids quieted. "Sharon volunteered to show us her hobby, which is a private and personal matter. This is a difficult thing for any of us. Your reaction is extremely rude."

Volunteered? thought Sharon.

Uneasily, Ms. Okashimo continued. "Sharon, perhaps you could tell us what you do with these paper dolls."

Somebody snorted but quickly swallowed the noise.

"Um . . ." Sharon muttered. "I lay them all out. I make up a story or . . . Most of the time I just go 'Eenie, meenie, minie, moe,' and the last one I count out dies, and I keep going until there's only one left. That one wins."

Laughter jumped out of the kids' throats. It bounced around the classroom walls. Sharon knew they couldn't help it. It was probably the best laugh they'd had in years.

Ms. Okashimo sounded slightly alarmed. "Thank you, Sharon."

"Excuse me?" asked a voice. "Could I ask a question?"

"Yes, Fern," Ms. Okashimo said dubiously.

Sharon frowned at the floor.

"What I'm wondering is why you play with paper dolls, Sharon?"

Someone snorted.

"Cut it out, Larry," Fern said.

Around Sharon, the class stopped its small sounds and movements. The only noise was the whir of the clock above the door.

"I'm not sure why I play with paper dolls. I know I'm too old for it. Maybe it's because it's just something to do. It helps me to stop thinking all the time. Sometimes, I think so fast and hard for such a long time that it hurts my head and I just want to stop."

The class sat very quietly. Sharon began to shove the paper dolls back into their envelope. She wasn't sure she could get back to her desk—the aisle seemed to have shrunk, so it felt much thinner than her big, stupid body. She tried not to bulldoze over any of the kids on her way back down the aisle.

"Coral, could you tell us about piloting an airplane now, please?" Ms. Okashimo asked.

Sharon shoved the envelope of paper dolls into her desk. She never wanted to see them again, but at least it was over now.

Coral was describing the controls of an airplane. Every now and then, Sharon glanced at the clock. The

hand was inching around—past 3:30, 3:40 . . . 3:42. The
bell rang. Around her, everyone was standing, getting out
their books, talking. Sharon sat and stared at her desk top.
She was going to sit there until absolutely everything else
that breathed left the room.

Chapter 5

"I don't know if that was such a very good idea," said a voice.

Sharon stared intently at her desk.

"I mean, Ms. Okashimo should never have made you do that," the voice continued. "I don't think that was fair at all."

Sharon chanced a sideways glance and saw the rubber boots. She decided to stand up and bumped her knee. "Ouch," she muttered.

"I mean about the paper doll presentation." Fern was still going on about it. Her wild, curly blonde hair shot out all over her head. Sharon felt as if her own hair hung down like a bunch of banana peels.

"I'm Fern," said the girl.

"I remember," said Sharon. She wondered what it'd be like to live in the middle of so much blonde curly hair.

"I think you live near me. Let's walk home together," said Fern.

Sharon tried to figure out how to get out of this. It'd just be the same old problem again. When she was by herself, she was constantly coming up with ideas—things to say, stories to tell. But when she saw another kid, the words got sucked into the Black Hole that lived in her brain. She was about as good at conversation as a turnip.

Fern didn't seem to be asking her. "Don't forget your paper dolls," she said.

Sharon picked up the envelope and followed the rubber boots as they clumped up the aisle. They walked out into the hall.

"Hey—there's Beetface! Beetface plays with paper dolls!"

Sharon began to slide off through the hall crowd, but she was yanked to a stop. Fern had her by the arm and had turned to face the speaker.

"I play with paper dolls," said Fern. "Paper dolls are great."

"Ah, c'mon, Fern. You do not," said the boy's voice. Sharon thought he was one of the ones who sat over by the window with the social success crowd. Fern sat with them in Science and Math.

"Sure I do," Fern said. "You don't know what you're missing, Jason."

"D'you fly airplanes too, Beetface?" jeered Jason.

"C'mon, Sharon." Fern's hand was now hauling Sharon down the hallway. "D'you need anything from your locker?"

"I don't think so," Sharon said, but she had no memories of life before the presentation. Her mind was a blank.

"Me neither. We're outta here." Fern kept a firm grip on Sharon's arm. The floor became a cement step, then asphalt. For a moment, Sharon stood blinking as her eyes adjusted to the afternoon sun.

Suddenly, someone burst out of the school doors behind them, bumping Sharon's shoulder. She had to take several steps to regain her balance and turned to see a boy

with dark skin and long black hair duck into a copse of
trees on the other side of the parking lot. He ran with a
bobbing motion, his body sinking down as he took each
step with his right foot.

"Keep out of the door!" he yelled, without turning
around.

"He's got a fake leg," said Fern.

Behind them, the girls heard more running in the
hall. Then a teacher stood panting in the doorway.

"You girls see anyone just now?" he asked. "An Indian kid?"

Sharon ducked her head.

"No. We've been out here for a while," said Fern.

Sharon sucked in her breath. The teacher shrugged
and went inside.

"Come with me, Sharon," said Fern. Her hand took
Sharon's arm again, and the rubber boots marched across
asphalt, a cement curb, grass, and another patch of asphalt.
The boots stopped. "We're in a parking lot. D'you ever
look up?"

"Not if I can help it," Sharon muttered.

The voice was grinning. "What if we got a tornado?
You wouldn't see it coming."

"I guess not."

Fern sat down on a curb. Why does this girl want to
talk to me? Sharon wondered. She has friends.

There was a scraping sound and the smell of sulfur.
Fern lit a match and watched the flame. She let it burn
close to her fingertips, then blew it out and lit another
one. They both watched the match burn down to Fern's
fingers. At the very last moment, Fern let it fall to the
pavement, then looked up and caught Sharon's eyes
watching through her hair. Sharon's eyes floated away.

"I like what you said . . . about the thinking?" Fern's voice stumbled over the words. "Sometimes, when I get thinking too much, I just turn off part of my brain, and I start counting things in a room, like the holes in the walls or the ticking of the clock—stuff like that."

Sharon sank down on the curb next to Fern. "Really?"

Fern gave her a quick corner-of-the-mouth grin and lit another match. "Yeah, really, Sharon. We're on the same planet. You think you were the only one?"

"But you don't play with paper dolls. I must be the only grade eight student in the entire country who still does that."

"Probably," Fern shrugged. "But see, I think I'm doing the same thing with these matches. Fire burns out your brain for a bit, and you stop thinking, right?"

Watching the flame did make her feel as if she were in a dream. "Sure," Sharon said.

"Ouch." Fern dropped the match. "I don't ever burn anything—I just watch it. I've been trying to figure out our teachers. They're like us—that's what I think."

This seemed impossible. "What d'you mean?"

"Well, you got your good ones and your mean ones. Okashimo's all right, really. Bohn's bad news. She's the Dark Side of the Force. I think the mean ones are mostly scared." Fern lit another match. "They're scared of us. Ever notice that?"

"Why would anyone be afraid of me?" Sharon asked.

"That's what I haven't figured out," Fern mused. "And about these paper dolls of yours, Sharon . . ."

Sharon tensed.

"I think you need a new hobby," said Fern. She grinned. "Switch to something else to stop from thinking—like TV."

"I guess," said Sharon.

"So, let's burn them," said Fern.

Burn them? Sharon stared down at the book of matches. Burn her paper dolls? Suddenly, they felt like part of her, part of her skin and bone. They were part of the hundreds, thousands of long, empty hours she'd spent lying on her bed, the paper figures stretched like a charmed circle around her, keeping things out of her head, keeping things at bay. "No," she said, placing the envelope on the other side of herself, away from Fern.

Sharon could feel the blue eyes on her and backed in behind her hair. There was the sound of another match being struck.

"Okay," said Fern. "Sounds like you live in Misselthwaite Manor."

A smile fluttered onto Sharon's face. *"The Secret Garden*—I read that."

"It was a good book. I read a lot," said Fern.

"Yeah?"

"Yeah." Fern lit another match.

Chapter 6

Uncle Bert had turned off all the lamps in the dining room. He sat on the sofa, the light from the TV making his face flicker in the dark. Sharon and her mother were cleaning up the supper dishes.

"Mom, d'you know much about Indians?"

"Indians?" Sharon's mother shot a nervous glance at Uncle Bert's ghostly face.

"There are some Indian kids at my school. There weren't any at my last school."

Sharon's mother's voice was so low Sharon had to stand close to hear it. "D'you mean Indians from India or Canada?"

"Canada. The ones in the First Nations."

In the next room, Uncle Bert shifted on the sofa and belched. Sharon watched her mother wince, then wring out the dishcloth, her knuckles white. Uncle Bert's voice came at them like a stabbing finger.

"You stay away from those welfare case kids, Sharon. They're all drunks and got lice. Want to steal our land with all their crazy land claims. Them boys'll want to take advantage of you. You'll end up like your mother."

Sharon stood as still as her mother, as still as the stacks

of dirty dishes on the counter, as still as the chairs, the table, the wall. Soap bubbles popped softly as water from the dishcloth dripped into the warm dishwater. Her mother seemed too quiet and frozen to be alive. Sharon glanced sideways toward the dining room. Uncle Bert was staring at the TV screen again, his face heavy and unmoving, as if he hadn't spoken a word.

I hate you, Sharon thought quickly.

Her mother moved again, dropped the dishcloth into the water. "Is your friend Fern an Indian?" she asked, not looking up.

"No."

"That's good," said her mother.

They finished the dishes in silence. Voices from the TV chatted and laughed in the next room. As she placed the dishes in the pantry cupboard, Sharon watched her mother stack and open files on the kitchen table. She'd go over the store accounts for an hour or so and then fade into the dining room like another shadow. There she'd watch TV from a corner of the room, jumping up to fetch Uncle Bert a coffee if he wanted it. This was what she'd done for Uncle Lawrence, too.

Sharon retired to her bedroom on the second floor. She emptied the envelope of paper dolls and spread them around her on the bed. "You'll end up like your mother," Uncle Bert's voice echoed in her head. He'd meant, of course, that her mother had gotten stuck being pregnant with Sharon. That's why she'd dropped out of high school. That's why she couldn't get a job now. Thinking was going on in Sharon's head again, and her brain hurt as if it were being beat up.

Downstairs, a door opened and feet came rapidly upstairs. Sharon's breath stopped. Her whole body held itself stiff and waited. Uncle Bert turned right and went on down the hall to the bathroom. Slowly, Sharon's body let itself relax.

"Just going to the can," she whispered to herself, her eyes skimming the paper dolls. "It's okay—it's not Uncle Lawrence."

They'd moved in with Uncle Lawrence when Sharon was in kindergarten because her mother had no money. Uncle Lawrence spent most of his time in front of the TV, a beer in his hand. His voice reminded Sharon of broken-down mufflers, and she'd tried to slide silently out of every room he came into.

Toward the end of the time they'd lived in his house, he began to yell at her mother every day. He bumped into walls and furniture more often, stumbling and swearing. When Uncle Lawrence acted this way, Sharon's mother would sit hunched, as if waiting for something to go away. She wouldn't look out of her eyes. She wouldn't say anything. Sharon's body did the same thing—tried to turn into a chair, a table, a rock—anything to not get noticed. She and her mother would stay this way until the yelling and banging stopped. Then they would start to move and breathe again.

One day in July, Sharon had been sitting at the kitchen table. Uncle Lawrence had stumbled into the kitchen toward her mother, who was standing by the sink. His hand had drawn back, then swung around and hit her mother's face. He'd pulled his hand back again, stepping forward.

Sharon didn't remember how it was that the table had gotten into her hands. Suddenly, she was full of hard, angry muscles, and she was shoving the table across the kitchen floor. It rammed against the small of Uncle

Lawrence's back. This had pushed Uncle Lawrence over the counter, next to her mother. All the plates and food on the table had slid off around the two adults, hitting them and crashing to the floor. There'd been the sound of Uncle Lawrence grunting softly and her mother crying.

Sharon remembered how the anger left her body. Her bones had become heavy and her feet stuck to the floor. For a long moment, no one had moved. Then her Uncle Lawrence had pushed his head under the tap and run cold water over it. He'd pulled his head out, dripping water all over the floor. "Get out," he'd said softly, then left the room. The next day, Sharon and her mother had caught a bus for Alberta.

Back in the present tense, Sharon heard Uncle Bert come out of the bathroom and go downstairs. She looked around at the bedroom she had in this house—the small flowers on the wallpaper, the dark floorboards, the dim overhead light that made things blur a little when it got dark outside. She didn't think about Rockwood much, didn't want to think about it. Most of the time, it was as if she'd never lived there, as if Rockwood and Uncle Lawrence had never been part of her life. Then there'd be a sound somewhere in the house—a creak on a stair, a door opening—and suddenly she'd see Uncle Lawrence coming at her, huge and angry. He'd be there just for a second. Then, like a flash, he'd be gone again.

On the bed, the faces of the paper dolls were all smiling at her, their eyes big and wide, without any worries. None of these paper faces had ever entertained a thought—that was obvious. Sharon reached for a black magic marker. Slowly and carefully, she colored a large black circle over the face of each paper doll, covering the stupid smiles, the empty eyes. When she'd finished, she slid them into the envelope and placed them at the back of her underwear drawer. Then she got out her well-thumbed copy of *The Lion, the Witch, and the Wardrobe.*

If only she had a closet that let her into distant lands on rainy days. She'd never come back.

Chapter 7

Sharon and Fern walked through the late September streets toward school. Fern wandered all over the sidewalk, following stones she kicked with her rubber boots. Sharon was worried. She'd been late leaving Uncle Bert's house because he had been yelling at her about the way she hung up her coat in the back hallway. Rushing along the street, she'd bumped into Fern, who'd been standing in front of someone's house, edging a stone out of the driveway with her boot toe. Now they were both close to being late for school. Sharon was trying to communicate this by walking quickly ahead of Fern and then pointedly waiting for the rubber boots to catch up.

Fern didn't seem to notice. Today, she wore cut-off jeans and an orange sweatshirt with green paint stains under her flapping jacket. Her hair was tied back with a red plastic bow clip. Fern was in her no-matching mood. She kicked at a tiny pebble with a kung fu yell, missed it, and tried again. Everything Fern did was in high gear, Sharon thought. She zoomed from one activity to the next. She was friends with everyone, best friends with no one. There didn't seem to be anyone Fern stopped talking around, no place she let herself go quiet . . . and think.

"Did you finish that grammar assignment?" Sharon asked.

"No." Fern veered off into a parking lot in pursuit of a stone.

"It was pretty long."

"I think it was dumb."

"Oh." Sharon hadn't thought having an opinion was part of the assignment.

Fern returned to the sidewalk. "I don't see the point. Underline the subject with one red line. Underline the verb with two green lines. Underline the object with a black wavy line."

Fern's latest stone shot off into traffic. She stopped, scanning for another. "Grammar this, grammar that. Why bother?"

"Oh." Sharon thought about this. "Most of the time, I feel like a dangling participle," she offered.

Fern whirled around, grabbing both of Sharon's shoulders. "That's it, Sharon! You're awesome!"

Sharon stared down and grinned the grin of a genius.

Fern booted another stone. "I wrote poetry last night —I'll hand that in for the grammar assignment."

"I think we should hurry," Sharon mentioned.

"Don't you want to hear my poem?"

Sharon could hear Fern laughing at her—it was there, rippling in her voice. A deep flush crept over her face, and she began to carefully observe sidewalk cracks.

"This is my poem." Fern stood still, one hand over her heart.

You take your shoes off when you walk into my mind
This ain't no highway and it ain't no Superstore
I don't want your army boots marching through my head
You take your shoes off and leave them by the door.

Fern laughed gleefully, then gasped. "Oh—there's a 7 Eleven. I gotta get a pop. Wait for me."

"We're late!" Sharon howled after her.

"It's breakfast," Fern yelled as she pulled open the door. Sharon waited. She couldn't just walk off and leave. Fern might get mad at her. Fern dashed out with two cans of pop.

"One for you," she said.

Through the school door, Sharon could see the office clock. It was a quarter after nine. Never before had she been late without an official mother-signed note.

"You're in for it," roared Uncle Bert in her head.

Fern pulled open the door and grinned, "After you."

Sharon stepped into the cool, dark hallway. Everyone was supposed to be on time, or else. "I guess we'd better . . ." she began.

"Shh," hissed Fern, clapping her hand over Sharon's mouth and pushing a good deal of hair between her lips. Pointedly, Sharon pulled the hand away, but Fern was now staring down the hall. Sharon turned to look.

The hall stretched out in front of them, sloping downward. At the other end, a classroom door was opening. As it did, Sharon noticed the boy leaning against the wall opposite the open door. His arms were crossed and his head was down, but she could tell it was the boy who'd bumped her the other day and then run off. The teacher who'd asked them about the Indian kid came out of the class and closed the door.

The teacher took three quick steps across the hall and grabbed the boy's shirt front with both hands. Then he lifted the boy slightly off the floor, up against the wall. The boy's head came up, and he glared back at the man. Fern's fingers tightened on Sharon's arm.

The teacher's voice came low but clear, up the hall. "Sometimes you make me so mad, I could put you through a wall."

The boy stared at the man, his feet hanging several inches off the floor. Dangling participle, Sharon thought.

"I guess that's *your* problem," the boy said.

"You push me any further, and I'll make it *your* problem," the teacher said, then let the boy drop so that he staggered slightly. "Detention, lunch and after school." The teacher walked to the class door and held it open.

The boy ignored him, brushing the front of his shirt, then straightened it with elaborate care. "Don't want to leave any incriminating evidence," he said. In his weaving movement, he walked into the classroom. The teacher followed him in and the door closed.

Softly, Fern said, "That's Ludlow—I heard about him from my brother."

"Geez, he wasn't too nice," Sharon said.

"Nice is not his hobby," Fern said.

Sharon was wondering if this was the treatment the school secretary dished out to late kids. "We have to go get our late slips right now," she insisted.

"Yeah, I guess."

Sharon followed Fern into the office, her eyes hitting the floor and staying put. Since Fern had made them late, she could do the talking.

"Good morning, ladies."

"We need late slips," said Fern.

"And your reason for being late?"

Sharon's fingers were leaving sweaty marks all over the counter. Not wanting to leave fingerprints, she tried to rub them out with the heel of her hand.

"I had to get a pop," said Fern. "It was my breakfast."

The lower half of the secretary's face looked highly unimpressed. "You had to get a pop?"

"Yes."

"And did you have to get a pop, too?"

Sharon swallowed. "No, I don't got a watch."

"Don't *have* a watch," said the secretary. "And that's not a good enough reason."

"We apologize for the inconvenience we may have caused you," said Fern.

"Next time a detention will inconvenience you." Two pink slips slid across the counter.

Sharon grabbed hers as if it were a lifejacket. "Thanks," she murmured. As they walked down the hall, she demanded, "How come you talked to her like that?"

Fern shrugged. "Felt like it."

"Oh."

"After you," said Fern, opening the classroom door.

Chapter 8

A series of early October rainy days had moved the lunch hour crowd indoors. Returning from a washroom trip, Sharon skirted the kids headed back to classes.

"Still playing with paper dolls, Beetface?" someone called.

Sharon felt the red take over her face and hurried on. From the doorway, she could see that almost everyone had left the cafeteria. It was five to one.

Empty tables stretched out in front of her. Panic oozed into Sharon's stomach. She remembered placing her retainer next to her lunch bag, but there was no sign of it anywhere. The panic was spreading now—down through her legs, up into her arms and throat. Her mother had no money. They never had any money, and when the dentist had told her mother that Sharon needed a retainer, her mother had turned a pasty white color. Sharon knew she'd never forget it.

I've got to find it, she thought.

"No money, no money," Uncle Bert hissed in her head.

She walked around each table. Then she crawled around under them. An apple core mashed to pulp under one of her hands. Maybe she'd put the retainer inside her lunch bag and someone, trying to be helpful, had thrown it into the garbage. Sharon scuttled out from under the table and stood up. There were two large gray pails. As she approached the closest one, the smell of rotting fruit greeted her. Sharon licked away some of the tears that had settled into the corners of her mouth.

The bags were soggy and tore in her hands. They were full of orange peels, smelly banana bruises, slimy pudding cups. One by one, Sharon pulled the bags out and piled them on the floor. Slowly, she stopped crying, though worry continued to sit in its heavy line across her stomach.

"Need some help?"

The boy's voice jumped through the air toward her. She'd thought she was alone. The Black Hole erupted in her head. When the blackness faded and the room came back, the boy was still there.

"I'm all right." Her hands kept pulling at the bags. She hoped this boy, whoever he was, would leave quickly.

Then another set of hands reached for a bag, opened it, and stopped. They were a warm brown color. The nails were chewed off. Sharon glanced up to about the middle of a black T-shirt.

"I'm looking for my retainer," she muttered.

"Okay."

It was the boy she and Fern had seen in the hall. They worked through the first pail, the only sounds those of tearing paper, the rattling of plastic spoons and cups. When the boy helped her dump the mess back into the garbage pail, his hands were covered with fruit cocktail.

"Pretty gross, eh?" he said, rubbing the guck off. "Makes you think you'll never be hungry again."

"Yeah." Sharon's brain had gone stupid. She stared down at her feet as if she'd suddenly discovered she had some.

"D'you want to do the other pail?"

She nodded.

"Okay," he said. "Why're you so upset?"

"We don't have any money. My mom'll be upset."

"We'll find it."

They started in on the second pail, not talking. Fear began to dull inside her. She felt very tired. Finally, the bottom of the pail was there, no retainer in sight.

"I guess we should put the stuff back," the boy said.

Sharon nodded again. The tears returned, softly running out of her eyes, down her face. She picked up a bag.

"No, don't worry—I'll do that," he said. "You just sit down."

Sharon forgot her face had been crying. She forgot about the banana mush she'd smeared across one cheek. For the first time, she looked straight at the boy's face. Surprise sucked air in through her mouth. There was an ugly purple hole where one of his eyes should've been. The one dark brown eye looked at her closely, its eyebrow frowning slightly. The boy ignored her gasp.

Probably used to it, she thought.

"You look real worried," he said.

The quiet room stretched out around the two of them. Everyone else was in class, hunched over their desks. Why was this boy standing here, not worried about the one hundred and one rules they were probably breaking?

"Why're you helping me?" she asked.

There was a pause. He swallowed hard, then shrugged. "I've lost . . . stuff. We should try Lost and Found. Maybe wash our hands before we go to the office, eh?"

Sharon laughed shakily. In the washroom, she scrubbed her hands and arms up to the elbows, keeping her head down to avoid the mirror. Then she washed her face. The boy was waiting in the hall. He looked at her and again Sharon found herself looking back. Why was this so easy? That empty eye socket sat in his face like a crater.

"You've got a nice face," he said. "Why d'you wear your hair over it like that?"

Sharon shrugged.

He grinned. "C'mon, let's go."

In the office, Sharon watched the secretary's lips press together. "What's the problem, Sharon?"

"I lost my retainer." Sharon observed the counter.

"Pardon?"

"My retainer," Sharon repeated. "I lost it."

"We thought it might be in the Lost and Found," said the boy.

"Are you involved with this, Richard Calliou?" snapped the secretary.

"He was helping me look," Sharon said quickly.

"Well, it's nice to see you involved in a positive activity, Richard." The secretary's tone softened. "There's no retainer in the Lost and Found though, Sharon. Where'd you lose it?"

"In the cafeteria."

"We'll keep an eye out for it." Two pink slips slid across the counter toward them. Sharon followed Richard's runners out of the office. In the hallway, the shoes stopped and turned toward her. They were torn at the sides.

"Sorry," he said awkwardly.

"It's not your fault."

"I know. It's just kind of cruddy. Maybe the janitor'll find it."

"Maybe."

Sharon could see her mother's face, white and upset. She turned and shuffled off to class. In her rush to sit down and get out of everyone's watching eyes, Sharon almost missed her seat.

"Psssst." It was Fern.

Sharon looked up. In Fern's outstretched hand sat her retainer. Relief exploded inside Sharon.

"You left it on the table," said Fern. "I didn't want it to get lost, so I took it with me."

"Oh." Sharon put the retainer in her mouth. For the rest of the afternoon, she kept her tongue tip pressed against the front wire just to make sure it was there.

Chapter 9

"This is the chamber pot," said Fern. "If you gotta go during the night, this is where you put it. We just got the outhouse in the backyard and it's too hard to find in the dark."

"Okay." Sharon observed the white pot. It should be easy to find in the dark, as long as she didn't mix it up with something else, like a garbage pail.

It was the Thanksgiving long weekend. Earlier that afternoon, Sharon had been at her locker, when Fern had suddenly turned on her and grabbed her arm. "Sharon!" she'd exclaimed. "What're you doing this weekend?"

Sharon had just heard Becky Manera say she couldn't go out to Fern's farm because her grandmother had died. She knew this was a secondhand invitation.

"Stuff." Aimlessly, she rummaged through her locker. "Homework."

"Playing with her paper dolls," Larry hooted.

"Go away, Knucklehead," Fern told him. She looked at Sharon encouragingly. "You could do homework at our farm."

"I dunno," Sharon hedged.

"Sharon." Fern sounded indignant. "You absolutely

cannot let me spend an entire long weekend *alone* with my mother."

Friday after supper, Fern's mother had driven the two girls out to the family farm. Fern's father was in Toronto on a business trip, and her older brother was out of town with his school band. It'd been dark by the time they arrived. Now the light of a kerosene lamp rounded the bedroom furniture with a yellow glow. A full moon seemed to take up half the window, and a quiver, gray-white like the moon, ran through Sharon. She sighed.

Fern jumped onto the bed, her hair a mass of gold lines in the lamplight. "D'you want to sleep on the left side or the right?" she demanded, bouncing.

"I don't care. Whatever you want."

"I knew you'd say that. I'll take the left. When I blow out this lamp, darkness will descend upon the earth."

"What about the moon?"

"It'll cloud over."

The two girls undressed, Sharon turning her back and pulling the nightgown over herself before she removed any clothing. This made it hard to get her shirt off, and she was sweating when she finished. When she turned around, Fern sat in her pj's, watching her.

"You're very shy about your bod."

Sharon had never changed in front of anyone else until this year's Phys. Ed. class. "Well, how d'you change?"

"Like that." Fern pointed at her jeans, shirt, socks, and underwear. She'd tossed them all over the room. "Just take it off and put it on."

Sharon's clothes were still in a lump around her feet. "Oh."

Fern bounced up and down again, slowly working her way beneath the sheets. Then she said, "Oops!" and rolled over and blew out the lamp. Blackness swooped in and surrounded them. Sharon stood in the darkness unable to see the bed, her toes curled up from the cold floor.

"Sharon?" called Fern.

Sharon walked forward into the end of the bed. "Ouch."

"It's a good idea to walk around the bed," advised Fern.

Sharon felt her way cautiously to one end of the bed, then up the side. Her hands curved around a bump.

"That's my foot. You're on my side," said Fern.

"Oh, sorry."

"Just climb over me."

Oh my goodness, thought Sharon. She could just see herself accidentally putting her knee into Fern's stomach or somewhere worse, and Fern getting really mad at her. "I'll go around." She felt her way down to the end and up the other side. Then she slid slowly between the sheets and held herself right at the edge of her side so that her face, elbows, and knees stuck out from under the quilt.

"Y'know, my mom and dad used to sleep in this bed," said Fern. She sounded a long way off. "Sometimes I wonder—y'know the Sex Ed. classes we get?"

"Yeah." Sharon's knees and elbows were getting cold. Slowly, she slid a bit farther under the quilt.

"Well, y'know that sperm stuff? Ever wonder if it gets out while they're sleeping?"

This conversation was making Sharon nervous.

"Well, y'see," continued Fern, "if it does, then it could get out into the bed, right? It could be here right now, crawling around."

Sharon gave a small shriek and curled her legs up under her.

"Well, what I wonder," said Fern, "is if that sperm might crawl inside us while we're asleep. We could get pregnant."

Sharon's arms and legs had her up and out of the bed before her next breath. She stood shivering in the dark.

"What's the matter?"

Sharon hugged herself and danced lightly on the cold floor. "I don't want to get pregnant," she hissed.

"Oh—I don't think you can, really." Fern was laughing. "I sleep in this bed lots, and I'm not pregnant."

"You'll end up like your mother," Uncle Bert warned.

Sharon stayed where she was.

Fern sighed. "You wearing underpants?"

Sharon was shocked. "Of course I am!"

"Then they couldn't get in anyway. Just get back in bed, okay?"

Sharon climbed in slowly and curled her legs up under her bum. She was sure Fern was no expert on sperm, but on the other hand she didn't want to have to sleep on the floor.

"Good." Fern sounded relieved. "You always this jumpy?"

"Sorry," muttered Sharon. Fern plumped her pillow and settled down. The darkness curved around them, shutting out everything but thoughts and voices. It was easier to talk this way.

"When I was three," said Sharon, "I remember thinking my mother got me by putting a quarter into a candy machine at a Kmart, and I dropped out instead of a handful of jelly beans."

"Really?" Fern rolled over onto her elbow. Sharon could feel the girl's breath against her arm.

"Yeah. Now I know I look too much like my mom to come from anywhere else."

"And your dad," Fern prompted.

Sharon hesitated. "I don't have a dad."

For once it was Fern who was quiet. "Oh," she said finally.

"I never had a dad. I mean, I know of course I have one somewhere, but I've never seen him. My mom won't tell me anything about him. If I ask her, she just looks away, so I don't ask anymore."

There was a pause, then Fern's arm patted her shoulder a couple of times.

"It's okay," she said to Fern. "I'm all right."

"Well, so who's that guy in the house you live in, then?"

"That's my Uncle Bert. Before this, we lived in this town called Rockwood with my Uncle Lawrence. We just moved out here this summer."

It'd been on her Uncle Lawrence's videos that Sharon had seen how people had sex. She wasn't supposed to be watching, but no one had noticed her standing in the doorway. She knew she must've happened that way.

"Why'd you move out on your Uncle Lawrence?" Fern asked. "Why'd you come to Alberta? I'd make Mom move to Vancouver."

Suddenly, Sharon was remembering a time just after she and her mother had moved in with Uncle Lawrence. She was five years old and sliding in her socks across her bedroom floor—back and forth, back and forth. Her flannel nightie billowed out with the speed she'd worked up so that she felt like a sailboat on a high sea. Then there was a sharp pain in the arch of her right foot. She slid to a halt, trying to keep that foot up off the floor and turned toward the bed to sit down.

That was when she heard feet coming up the stairs, loud and fast. The door to her room burst open and

Uncle Lawrence was coming in, yelling about too much noise. Sharon stood, her weight on her left foot, trying to keep her right foot up on tiptoe so the sliver wouldn't touch the floor. She couldn't run, couldn't move as he came toward her, and then he had her by both arms and she was up in the air. She landed on the bed, her head hitting the wall.

Uncle Lawrence slammed the door when he went out again. She sat on the edge of the bed, her face numb and still as a doll's, turning her right foot up so that she could see the sole. The sliver stuck out through the sock in the arch of her foot. It was thick and about as long as her finger. Without blinking, she'd pulled it out, then held her thumb over the hole to slow the flow of blood into her sock.

The memory was gone as suddenly as it'd come. Sharon lay still for a moment, trying to remember what Fern had asked her.

"You all right?" Fern asked. "You're so quiet."

"I'm okay," Sharon said. "Guess Mom wanted a change."

"Tired of the same old place?"

"Yeah," said Sharon and left it at that.

Chapter 10

Sharon lay for a long time in the dark, trying not to think about Uncle Lawrence. She counted blank, smiling paper-doll faces in her head. Beside her, Fern's sleepy breathing went on and on. Sharon realized she had to use the washroom. She'd have to find that chamber pot Fern had pointed out.

The floor was so cold. It made her have to pee worse. Sharon danced quietly on the floor. Where was that thing? It was so dark that she was going to have to find it by touch. Sharon moved all the way around the edge of the bed, quietly shuffling up and down Fern's side. No pot here, she thought. She barked her shin. The pain that chewed into her bone felt so bright that she was surprised it didn't light up the whole room. Softly, she groaned and waited for it to go away.

The best thing to do would be to continue on her hands and knees. This would get her very cold feet up off the floor and relieve her bladder. Sharon crawled forward slowly, feeling with her hands for the pot. That'd been really dumb, not getting Fern to tell her where she'd put it.

"Idiot!" roared Uncle Bert.

The bladder situation had gotten worse. Sharon's head connected with some furniture. There didn't seem to be a way around it on her hands and knees. She stood up and found a narrow space to slide through. Then she bumped into something that felt like a chair. Probably, Fern had put the pot on the other side.

By now, her bladder was in a crisis state. There was no time to waste tiptoeing around things. She climbed onto the chair and felt beyond it. There was something there too, and she climbed up onto that. Behind it, she felt space and she slid down into it, intending to move on in search of the invisible chamber pot.

But she couldn't move. Halfway down into the space, she'd felt something behind it—smooth and taller than herself. All around her, dark shapes loomed, closing her in. She was stuck.

"Fern?" she hissed softly.

There was a moan and a soft shifting on the bed, but no answer.

"Fern?" Sharon called again. A sharp pain stabbed at her groin.

"Sharon?" Fern's mouth was full of sleep. "What's the matter?"

It started. The hot flow forced its way out. Sharon tried, but there was no stopping it. It rushed down her legs and onto the floor.

"Where are you, Sharon?" The bed squeaked as Fern sat up.

"I dunno," said Sharon, "but I think I just peed all over your floor."

The springs squeaked again as Fern got out of bed.

"I think you'd better put on your boots," Sharon added.

Fern banged into a few things.

"I think there's a lot of stuff in the way," Sharon apologized.

"How'd you get all the way back there?" Fern asked.

"I dunno."

"I'll go get a flashlight. Don't go away." The boots clumped off.

Very funny, thought Sharon. Don't go away. She shifted her feet in the cooling puddle. Then she saw the light coming down the hall. Fern played the light over the room. Sharon watched the beam stretch out, advance in sudden bounces and jumps over several chairbacks, a desk, then over the top of a dresser. The light hit her eyes.

"You're behind the dresser!" Fern said in awe. "How'd you get there?"

Suddenly, there was a flurry of laughter in Sharon's stomach. "I think I was trying to get away from the sperm," she gasped.

Fern's flashlight started to bob up and down as laughter grabbed her, too. They laughed so hard and long it hurt, and it hurt all the more because they were trying to keep quiet.

"Well, let me get you out." Fern shifted the chair and then the dresser. "You looked so funny with the top of your head poking over the dresser," she giggled. "I could even see your eyes. Your hair's out of your face."

With her free hand, Fern reached out and pushed some of Sharon's hair to one side. Fear flicked across Sharon. She stepped back, but Fern's hand held onto her hair.

Sharon's eyes flicked away, then back, away, then back. The flashlight made deep, shadowy caverns out of both their faces. One of Fern's eyes looked like an empty socket, and her nose loomed huge on her face. Distorted, half there, her face was easier to look at. They stood in silence, observing each other.

"Welcome to the universe, Hairy Nymph of the Dresser," Fern said solemnly.

"Thank you, O Mistress of the Chamber Pot," Sharon replied.

They cleaned up Sharon and the puddle, and Fern gave her another nightgown to wear. Sharon pulled out a clean pair of underwear. "For protection," she said, waving it in the air. Fern giggled.

"By the way," Sharon asked once they'd climbed back into the bed and bounced around to make the springs squeak. "Where did you put that stupid chamber pot?"

"Under the bed, of course. So no one would kick it over."

The giggles grabbed them again, so they had to stick their heads under the covers and shriek, soundless, into the quilt.

Chapter 11

Ms. Bohn had divided the Home Ec. class into groups of three or four, which rotated through different sewing and cooking activities. Sharon and Fern had been placed together with Frank Giles, who had fallen sloppily in love with Fern and ignored Sharon. This was fine with Sharon. Today, their group was cooking pudding. Fern was at the stove, stirring, while Frank, who had dishwashing duty, admired her.

Sharon had opted for the table-setter's job. She'd noticed Ms. Bohn didn't pay much attention to this person, only inspecting the table once it'd been set. Sharon had checked to ensure all the cutlery was clean. Nervously, she arranged and rearranged it on the place mats.

"Why don't you turn the forks upside down?" Fern asked as she stirred. "Just for variety or something."

One of the rules stated that the cutlery and plates were to be placed exactly two centimeters from the table's edge. Sharon sweated over the ruler, trying to remember if the black border that lined the edge was part of the first centimeter, or if the first centimeter started after it.

"Did you wipe off the chairs?" demanded Ms. Bohn.

"No, ma'am," Sharon said, staring down.

"Get into the habit, Sharon. It's sanitary." The black shoes marched off.

"Hey, Sharon."

Sharon turned. Fern was standing at the counter, screwing the lid back onto a jar of sweet and sour pickles. She winked, tapped her own right shoulder, then pointed to Ms. Bohn. There was a small, round, green pickle slice riding Ms. Bohn's right shoulder.

Frank snickered. Sharon saw some of the kids grinning at Ms. Bohn's back. Fern chewed ferociously on her gum. Sharon waited for Ms. Bohn to notice. She waited for the teacher to start yelling and throw the pickle slice. Ms. Bohn didn't. All that happened was that Fern swore softly and began to hack at lumps forming on the bottom of the pot.

It was the best pudding Sharon had ever eaten. Fern had placed a pickle slice on top of each one.

"Sharon." Fern had kept her gum wad on the bottom of her pudding bowl and returned it to her mouth with the last spoonful. "You let Ms. Bohn get so big in your brain, there's no room left for you."

Sharon looked at her almost empty pudding bowl. "It's her classroom."

"But it's your brain," Fern pointed out. *"Die denken sind frei."*

"I don't get it," said Frank.

"Thoughts are free. It's from a Jean Little book," Fern explained.

"From Anna," contributed Sharon.

"So what if you don't agree with a teacher all the time?" said Fern. "You're not blowing up the school. It's not a crime."

"She'll get mad."

"So?" Frank asked.

"So she gets mad," said Fern. "She can't keep mad forever."

"Well, what if she gives you a detention?" Sharon asked.

"So you get a detention," Fern shrugged.

"Well, what if they kick you out of school?" Sharon said.

"They're not gonna kick you out of school," Frank snorted.

"You, Sharon Frejer," said Fern, waving her spoon, "would never do anything in your entire life that'd get you kicked out of school."

Frank snorted again. Sharon wasn't sure she liked Fern's tone, but she considered the idea. All her life, she'd assumed that you had to agree with adults on everything. *Everything.* Adult disapproval meant . . .

Well, what does it mean? Sharon pondered. Thoughtfully, she spooned the last of the pudding out of her bowl.

Chapter 12

"That's him!" Fern said.

It was recess. Sharon followed Fern's stare and saw Richard Calliou leaning against one of the trees out behind the teacher's parking lot. He was smoking. He hadn't even bothered to stand behind one of the bare-branched trees.

A cold gust of wind blew Sharon's hair out and away. There was something about the way Richard was all tight lines and sharp bones, like the late-October trees around him, that held Sharon, kept her still. That cold, harsh face couldn't possibly belong to the boy who'd groped through two garbage pails of slop looking for her retainer.

"Excuse me." Fern walked straight over to Richard. Sharon followed, tiny fingers of surprise flicking around inside her chest.

Richard didn't respond to Fern. Sharon looked up into the pause to find he was watching her instead.

"Find your retainer?"

The wind was also after his long hair. Sharon felt it happening again—her eyes made that simple, easy lift and she was looking into his face. A glad smile washed through her.

"Yeah," she said. "My friend Fern here took my retainer to class so I wouldn't lose it. I'm sorry I wasted your time like that."

"Don't worry about it. Got me out of class." In a sudden gust of wind, his cigarette went out. He swore softly, then turned his back to the wind, cupping his body around the cigarette to relight it.

Sharon hadn't told Fern about the garbage pail incident. For some reason, she'd wanted to keep it for herself. Now she ignored Fern's inquiring poke in her ribs. "Thanks again," she said.

"Anytime." He sucked on the cigarette and the lines of his face became harsher, turned him into someone else. Glancing down, she saw his feet in brilliant white runners kicking into the dirt. "New runners," he muttered, following her eyes. "Staff just got them for me. Gotta break them in so I don't look like a geek."

"Excuse me," Fern repeated.

"Yeah?" Richard moved so he could see Fern, who stood facing his empty eye socket. Sharon watched his smile drain away.

Fern was examining the eye socket with quick runaway glances. "Sharon and I were late for school about two weeks ago, and we saw what happened—well, with you and Ludlow in the hall."

"So?"

"Well, that's not allowed. Ludlow's not supposed to do that. I think we should go talk to the principal."

Richard leaned against a poplar and laughed, his head bumping back so that his Adam's apple moved up and down sharply. "Yeah, right," he said. He sucked on the cigarette and stared off across the school grounds.

Fern reddened. "We'll be your witnesses. We'll go to

the principal. He'll have to do something about it."

"He won't do anything," scoffed Richard.

"My dad's a lawyer, and I know what Ludlow did is against the law," Fern protested.

Richard blew out smoke in a long, narrow line. "I won't be here for long."

Sharon felt shut out. She knew she didn't own Richard, but suddenly, all over herself, she didn't want him to give Fern that same gentle look he'd given her. That smile was hers. And she wanted in on this conversation. She shoved her hair impatiently aside. "What d'you mean?"

"They moved me through three schools last year," he said. "I live in group homes, see? Or foster homes. Right now, I'm at the Youth Center. I figure I've got a coupla months here at most." He looked at Fern. "Principals know my type, so they don't do nuthin'."

"Don't you even want to try?" Fern asked.

Richard stared up through the tree branches overhead, his chin a sharp line in his skin. It was very quiet.

"Why'd you come over here, Fern?" Richard's question was abrupt. "Think I need your help or something?"

Fern's chin went up stiffly. "What's the matter with wanting to help?"

The school buzzer rang. Richard straightened and dropped the cigarette on the ground.

"You helped me," Sharon said suddenly.

Richard continued to stare at his blazing white runners.

"Okay," he said finally. "We'll go see Mr. Principal. Though it'll just be pissin' in the wind."

Then he reached into his pocket and pulled something out. Eyebrows raised, his one dark eye watched them. He put a hand over the eye socket and pushed something into it. When he pulled his hand away, there was a glass eye staring at them. "They won't let me in unless I'm dressed properly."

If her life had depended upon it, Sharon could not have kept her mouth closed. A strange, wild laugh came out of her. Surprised by the sound, she started to look away. Richard grinned.

"Do I look better this way, Sharon?"

"I'm not sure." She wanted to say the glass eye didn't change the rest of his face at all, that in some way she preferred the empty socket because . . . why? Because she was weird. "No," she said finally. "I . . . I like your face."

But maybe he hated his face with an empty socket. He must think her rude for saying that. Stupid.

"Stoopid!" roared Uncle Bert.

"Thanks, Sharon." Briefly, an arm went around her shoulders and tightened. Sharon felt her eyes swell, and she stared fiercely at the ground.

"Guess we'd better get going," said Fern.

The arm, its warmth, slid away.

"After you," Richard said.

"We're going to the principal?" Fern insisted. "After school?"

"Sure," Richard said.

"Sure," Sharon echoed.

Chapter 13

"What would you like?" The secretary had matched her tone to her frown.

"We'd like to see the principal," said Fern.

It was after school. Sharon had decided to remain behind as much of her hair as possible. Fern was attempting to sound as if she consulted with the principal on a daily basis, but Sharon could see the way her right foot had lifted off the floor and was moving up and down the lower back of her left leg. The toes of Richard's runners knocked against each other. Across their sanitary white surface, a few swear words had been inked in. They hadn't been there at recess.

"Mr. Sidlowski is a very busy man," said the secretary. "Is this important?"

No, we'd just like to develop a useless habit of coming and asking to see the school principal, thought Sharon, then wondered in alarm where the thought had come from. Fern must be taking over her head.

"Very important," Fern said calmly.

"What may I tell him it's about?"

"It's sort of private."

Fern's right foot slid down her leg and began to tap

against the floor. Richard's toes knocked together at a frantic pace.

"Ah, c'mon—you know it's about me," said Richard abruptly.

"I'd assumed that, Richard," said the secretary. "I'll see if Mr. Sidlowski is free."

Heels clicked off across the floor. In the quiet office, Sharon listened to the other two breathing. The heels came clicking back. "Mr. Sidlowski says he has ten minutes."

Sharon followed Fern through a doorway and onto a brown carpet.

"Hello. Why don't you sit down?" Mr. Sidlowski got up from the desk and closed the door. Sharon dove into a nearby chair and settled in behind her hair as the principal crossed the room and sat down in his chair.

Fern's hands were folded in her lap. Richard's gripped the two arms of his chair. Sharon's were in fists, hiding dirty fingernails.

"What can I do for the three of you?" The principal sounded friendly enough.

"Well, actually, Mr. Sidlowski . . ." Fern's voice was higher than usual. "Sharon and I saw something we wanted to complain about."

"Oh? Well, I'd be interested in hearing about it," said Mr. Sidlowski. "I assume this must have something to do with Richard? Hello, Richard."

"Hi." Richard jerked the sound out of his throat.

Fern's words came out quickly. "Sharon and I were late one morning last week. We came into the school, and we saw Richard standing down the hall." She paused.

"Go on," said Mr. Sidlowski.

The principal's tone changed, as if tightening its grip.

Sharon was watching his hands. They were white, the fingers very long. The principal kept weaving his fingers together—in and out, in and out.

"Well . . ." Fern sounded hesitant, unsure of what to say next. "Well, we saw a classroom door open and a teacher came out. He came across the hall to Richard, and he shoved him up against the wall. Really hard! He lifted him off the floor! He said Richard made him so mad, he felt like putting him through a wall."

Mr. Sidlowski's fingers hesitated, then continued their movement. He said nothing.

Sharon looked from Mr. Sidlowski's hands to Richard's. The boy had tightened his grip on the chair. She could see the tendons outlined in his hands.

"I think that was mean," said Fern. "I don't think that was right."

There was another pause.

"I see," Mr. Sidlowski said. "I can see that what you saw would concern you. I'm sure there must be some sort of misunderstanding."

Sharon heard Richard let his breath out in a very quiet laugh. His hands relaxed their grip on the chair.

"I don't think we could've misunderstood," said Fern slowly.

Mr. Sidlowski's hands stopped for a moment, then continued. "I suppose I'm not convinced of that, Fern. Now Richard, what was the name of this teacher?"

"Peter Ludlow." Richard said the teacher's first name easily, almost as a put-down. He leaned back against the chair, his one dark eye watching Mr. Sidlowski casually, as if the man were unimportant, part of a passing crowd.

It's a dare, Sharon thought. Richard was daring Mr. Sidlowski to call him on this inappropriate use of words.

Mr. Sidlowski's fingers were gripping one another tight-ly. There was another pause.

"Well, why don't I talk to Mr. Ludlow? See if I can clear up this . . . misunderstanding of yours." The hands began moving again, sliding smoothly around themselves, then grabbing the wrists. For a moment, Mr. Sidlowski looked as if he were handcuffing himself.

"Well . . ." Fern sounded as if she wasn't sure whether she'd gotten what she wanted. "Okay. Should we come back and talk to you again later?"

Mr. Sidlowski's tone lost its friendliness. "Fern, I'll certainly talk to you if there's a need to do so. Thank you for coming in and expressing your concerns."

"Oh," said Fern. "Thank *you,* Mr. Sidlowski."

"Well, and thank you," said Mr. Sidlowski. "Just let me write your names down. Fern Thompson. Sharon . . . ?"

"Sharon Frejer," Sharon whispered.

"And Richard Calliou," finished Mr. Sidlowski. "Have a good day."

Out in the hall, Richard turned and looked at them. "There," he said. "You happy?" He was looking at Fern, a small grin on his lips, the rest of his face stretched tight.

"Happy?" repeated Fern.

"I hope so," Richard said. "We did that for you. It sure as hell ain't going to do me any good."

Sharon stared at him.

"What d'you mean?" asked Fern.

"He'll tell Ludlow and I'll get more shit, but I knew that when I went in there. Just thought it'd be good for you Mother Teresa types to find out what it's like."

He turned and walked down the hall in his odd, bob-bing walk. Behind him, silence filled up the hallway. It moved out over the playground and across the whole city, coming from nowhere and everywhere like the wind.

He hadn't done this to teach them a lesson. Sharon remembered his feet, twisting around each other like newborn puppies. It had been hope that had taken him into the principal's office, just like them.

Chapter 14

Sharon stood next to Fern at one of the stoves in the Home Ec. classroom, trying to figure out a rhyme for "Bunsen burner." Fern was working on a poem for science class. Frank was absent. This left the two girls making cookies. Sharon had just finished setting the table.

"You take your shoes off when you walk into my mind," Fern sang softly, bobbing her head about and tossing in random blues notes. "How's this for the law of gravity?" she asked suddenly. Raising the box of baking soda about two feet above the counter, she poured some into the bowl.

Sharon giggled, then grabbed a dishcloth and wiped up the soda that had missed the bowl. A quick check told her Ms. Bohn hadn't noticed. She was involved with David Pham's sewing project. He was making pot holders out of a fabric with hockey players on it. Fern proceeded to dump sugar into the bowl without measuring it.

"I don't know about this," Sharon said.

"Live a little, Sharon," Fern snapped. She backed up a few steps. "Let's just see what she thinks about this," she muttered and began tossing chocolate chips one by one into the bowl.

Ms. Bohn came at them like a tidal wave, slamming the recipe book down on the counter.

"Oh, Ms. Bohn!" said Fern, her voice like a thin, bright wire. "I didn't see you."

Sharon was hoping Ms. Bohn had noticed that she had been nowhere near the package of chocolate chips. The muscles in Ms. Bohn's face had sucked her mouth in so far that it'd almost disappeared. The teacher walked up to Fern, placed a hand on each of her shoulders, and pushed her slowly back to the bowl of cookie batter.

"This is where we stand, dear," she said. "D'you think you can manage this?"

As her face reddened, Fern said, "Y'know, I think this will help, actually. I'm supposed to wear glasses."

Ms. Bohn's hands tightened briefly on Fern's shoulders. "Report for detention after school," she said and walked back to the sewing machines.

Sharon stood pushing a finger back and forth over the same centimeter of counter top until the friction caused a burning sensation. She refused to look at Fern.

"Pass me that knife."

"What?" asked Sharon.

"Pass me that knife." Fern was digging the tip of the spoon against the bottom of the bowl in mechanical jabs. "I've got to cut off a quarter cup of lard. Ms. Bohn stuck my feet to the floor right here, right in front of the cookie bowl. I'm never allowed to move from here again—ever, ever, ever—and I can't reach that knife from here."

They regarded each other silently. Fern's grin looked as if she'd taped it onto her mouth. Behind it, Sharon felt a coldness, something that pushed her away. Today, that something in Fern was pushing everyone away. Sharon's eyes dropped, and her hand floated over to the small, sharp knife lying on the counter.

Fern took it from her in a delicate, mocking gesture. Dramatically, she sliced the block of lard. Then a look of bright shock flashed across her face. The knife clattered to the counter.

"Ouch!" Fern cried. She lifted her finger and sucked it.

Ms. Bohn looked up from the pot holders. Sharon drifted, faded, vanished around to the other side of the counter, wanting to put as much space as possible between herself and the approach of Ms. Bohn.

"Ow," Fern whimpered.

Ms. Bohn grabbed the bloody finger. "What's the problem here?"

"My finger," Fern said. "I cut it."

"Why were you using a knife to make cookies?" demanded Ms. Bohn. She shoved Fern's finger under the tap and ran water over it.

"I had to cut the lard."

Ms. Bohn wrapped a dishcloth around the finger. "Go see the nurse."

"Yes, Ms. Bohn," Fern chirped. Turning to go, she winked at Sharon.

"And you can both report for detention after school. That includes you, Sharon," said Ms. Bohn. She turned to go back to the pot-holder project.

Sharon felt a small earthquake rattle the classroom floor. A detention?

"Why is Sharon getting a detention?" Fern asked.

"I saw that wink. You two are a bad influence on each other," said Ms. Bohn.

"She didn't do anything," stammered Fern. "I just winked at her. Honest."

"Go to the nurse, Fern." Ms. Bohn's voice had become very loud. Fern scuffed off. "You finish those cookies now, Sharon."

As the door closed behind Fern, Sharon picked up the wooden spoon and stared at the batter. At the other end of the counter, Ms. Bohn stood and watched. Sharon stirred, peering down through her drooping hair. She had to be careful to get this absolutely right. What if she stirred wrong and the bowl ended up on the floor? The rest of the class was very quiet. Sharon spooned the cookie dough onto the sheets. Ms. Bohn stood there watching until Sharon set the cookies into the oven. Then she returned to the sewing group. Sharon set the timer. She began to wash dishes. Here was another reason to be mad at Fern, who was off getting a Band-Aid and some sympathy. Anger bubbled in her stomach, cooking away like all those cookies. She checked the timer. The cookies were almost ready to eat.

"I'm going to see what's taking Fern so long," Ms. Bohn announced. "Get on with your work, everyone." She left the room.

As the door closed, Sharon's arm reached over and turned off the timer. The arm just stretched out, on its own, the fingers taking hold of the timer and turning it off. She returned to washing dishes. As the smell of burning cookies began to drift through the air, Sharon concentrated on rinsing each dish so that every single soap sud floated off. She stacked them, making sure they didn't clink against each other, picked up a tea towel, and with extreme care began to dry the bowl off. All around her, the room was completely silent, except for the whir of the sewing machines. Every now and then, someone glanced at her and sniffed, but no one said a word.

White smoke began to wisp, then drift out of the oven. Sharon watched it out of the corner of her eye. A shaking had started up inside her. What was she doing? Nothing. If nothing was what got you into trouble, then let it.

Sharon kept shaking as she dried each cooking utensil. She dried some plates and utensils twice. The smoke alarm went off. No one moved. When Ms. Bohn dashed back into the classroom, she saw everyone bent silently over sewing projects and Sharon placing the dish rack under the sink.

The smoke was now black and pouring out. Ms. Bohn ran over, turned off the oven and opened the oven door. She grabbed a pot holder and pulled the cookie sheet out, dumping the cookies into the sink, then ran cold water over the black, withered mess. She stood waiting for the alarm to stop.

The sudden silence was louder than the alarm.

"Stand out in the hall until the end of class, Sharon Frejer. Double detention in this room after school."

Sharon walked quietly past the teacher, careful not to brush against her. She scuffed past the kids at the sewing machines and tables, not looking at anyone. She pushed open the Home Ec. door and walked into the long, cool hallway. Close by was the door to the front office. Teachers and students came and went. Sharon leaned against the wall, then slid to the floor. Trouble was coming after her, and this time she'd asked for it.

"Stoopid!" roared Uncle Bert.

Trouble, Sharon thought. Big trouble. She felt dizzy. The school hallway faded out, and a different scene flashed across the inside of her head. She was in her pj's, maybe nine years old, in her Rockwood bedroom. Her tall, white dresser had been shoved across the door, a mirror knocked down and smashed on the floor. She was pulling her bed out from the back corner, then across the floor, shoving and pushing until it rested behind the dresser.

The doorknob rattled. Someone began to yell and bang on the door, pushing against it. It was Uncle Lawrence. In the memory, Sharon turned and headed for her desk. She wanted to drag it over, try to heave it up onto the bed for extra weight, but she was only halfway across the room with the desk when her uncle rammed the door open. The bed slid toward her, against her knees, trapping the small of her back against her desk. She couldn't move, couldn't get away.

The scene faded. Back in the school hallway, Sharon was very careful not to see anyone walk by. She pulled her knees up and sat in a tight triangle. For the rest of the period, she counted and recounted the threads that ran across the worn kneecaps of her jeans.

Chapter 15

Sharon stood outside the Home Ec. door. All afternoon, she'd refused to speak to Fern. All afternoon, she'd kept her eyes down or on her work. Everything that'd happened that morning was because of Fern Thompson. It was all her fault—the burnt cookies, Ms. Bohn's being angry, Sharon's detention.

Now Sharon heard rubber boots clumping down the hallway. Without looking up, she pushed through the half-open door. Ms. Bohn stood up behind her desk.

"Sharon?" she said, pointing dramatically to the burnt, soggy mess still in the sink. Sharon scuffed over and began to clean up the cookie sheet. Fern was told to sweep the floor. They worked without speaking. Ms. Bohn's pencil scratched over the tests she was marking. Fern's broom swished and jabbed. Sharon's cleaning pad scraped against the cookie sheet. When she'd rinsed and dried the pan, Sharon stood silently, not wanting to break the silence. Words could bring *anything* with them.

Ms. Bohn raised her thin face. "Yes, Sharon?"

"I'm finished."

Ms. Bohn checked the pan, then handed her a paper

and a list of the Home Ec. rules. "Write these out ten times," she ordered.

Grateful, Sharon began to write. Filling up a blank paper with made-to-order sentences was just the kind of thing she was good at. Never in her entire life—*never*—would she burn another cookie. Quickly, she wrote the words out neatly across the page: *Students must have permission to use the sewing machines.*

When Fern finished sweeping the floor, she was also given the list of rules to write out.

As Fern sat down opposite, Sharon turned away to the left, so that she saw as little as possible of her. Still, she could see Fern's pale face glancing at her. Finally, Ms. Bohn leaned over Sharon's shoulder and said coldly, "You may go now."

Sharon pushed up from the table and walked quickly out of the room and down the hallway. She twirled her combination lock so fast she had to redo it three times before she got it right, then stuffed herself into the orange ski jacket her mother had bought on sale. It looked like it. Every time Sharon moved, the coat gave off cheap rustling sounds. As she pushed out into the early November cold, slivers of wind slid in at the seams.

Snow had already come to stay, but she'd been in too much of a rush to change to her boots. Quickly, her feet were wet and cold in her canvas runners. Sharon kicked at a chunk of ice. Finally, she understood why Richard didn't like Fern.

Richard. Sharon hadn't talked to him since their visit to Mr. Sidlowski's office. He didn't come into the cafeteria much. From a distance, she'd seen him leave the school grounds, shoulders curved against the wind. There was something about him that always seemed to belong to loneliness.

"Sharon!"

It was Fern behind her, running to catch up. Sharon took off down a side street.

"Stoopid!" roared Uncle Bert.

Sharon ran through the gray afternoon, a bright orange ball of rage. She didn't notice when Fern stopped calling, when the sound of feet behind her faded, but when she came to a halt in Uncle Bert's driveway, she was alone.

Alone—that's what she wanted. Alone and invisible. Sharon climbed the stairs to her bedroom, hanging onto the railing. She closed the door, pushed at it to make sure it clicked completely shut.

This afternoon, she needed them again. From her closet, Sharon took out the shoe box with the remaining paper dolls—the ones whose faces she hadn't blacked out. Spread out on the bed in rows, there were about seventy left. They smiled up at her. Cracks and bends ran through their faces and bodies. She'd had some of them for eight or nine years.

Quietly, mechanically, she began the game. Her voice was soft and monotonous, like the ticks of a clock. "Eenie, meenie, minie, moe," she chanted softly. "Catch a monkey by the toe." Around her, the paper doll game closed in, quiet, safe. Slowly, the fear washing through her settled, then disappeared. She was close to the nothingness she wanted, the no-thinking place.

One of the magazine figures gave her an especially stupid look.

"Eenie, meenie, minie, moe." Sharon couldn't stop.

Chapter 16

Sharon wanted to talk to Fern every time she saw her. Her heart would speed up, words crowding together inside her head. Sometimes, their eyes would meet and hold. But then Sharon would turn away. Fern had made her get into trouble. She'd made Sharon act different than before. It scared Sharon. She returned notes Fern passed to her in class unopened. She brought books to school to read at recess and lunch hour.

After a week, Fern stopped trying to get her attention. Her voice changed, became harsher, louder. She started to hang around with a group of boys. Sharon watched them leave the school grounds at lunch. She wanted to run after Fern, say the right thing, but she knew she'd left it too long. Fern would look at her like a stranger and laugh loudly. She'd probably just been putting up with Sharon all along.

November was a lonely month. In the last week, Sharon watched Fern push open an exit door with Len Razlaff, then turned toward the cafeteria with her lunch. Inside the doorway, her eyes jumped from table to table of shouting, laughing kids. Sometimes she sat with several girls who bussed in from the country, but she didn't see them anywhere. In the back right corner, she spotted a table that had only a few kids and, with his back to a wall, Richard Calliou. He sat, his feet up on the bench, tossing his glass eye from hand to hand. She watched it go up and down, up and down, higher on each toss.

Sharon stood for a moment, trying to imagine herself walking up to him in that comfortable, relaxed way other kids walked up to each other. When they did it, it looked easy.

"Stay away from that kid!" boomed Uncle Bert.

"I'm glad your friend Fern's not an Indian," said her mother.

Sharon brushed the hair back from her face. Then she made herself walk forward and turn down the aisle next to Richard. She kept her eyes on the table. He was coming into view—his black T-shirt, the shoulders. She saw the glass eye land in the hand and stay there, staring at her.

"Hi, Sharon."

He was smiling. She dropped down onto the bench on the opposite side of the table.

"I like your hair like that."

"Thanks." Sharon forced herself to put her elbows on the table and her chin on her hands. His gaze was on her face, moving over her forehead, eyes, mouth, chin. Would he decide she was ugly and look away?

"So what happened to you?" He was still smiling.

Sharon figured he meant he could see her face. "Just wanted a change, I guess."

"Oh. Where's your Siamese twin?"

Fern had been her friend, a real friend. Sharon didn't want to think about it. "I guess we sort of had a disagreement."

Richard laughed. "You mean a fight?"

"Yeah." Sharon began to open her lunch. "We looked for you after that meeting with Mr. Sidlowski, but we couldn't find you. Did Ludlow go after you again?"

Richard started tossing the eye. "Believe it or not, the old guy apologized to me. Sidlowski was there. Bet Ludlow had to do it or lose his job."

Sharon took out her retainer and reached for her lunch bag.

"No, wait!" Richard's hand shot across the table toward her. "Let me take care of that. I'm not going through any more garbage pails." Carefully, he picked up the retainer and put it into his jacket pocket.

Sharon smiled. It looked as if he actually expected her to sit there for a while. What should she say next? "So is Ludlow treating you any better?"

"Well, y'see . . ." Richard swung around so that he was facing her. "He didn't admit he'd pushed me against the wall or threatened me. In fact, he said I was lying about that. But he did say his temper had gotten a little out of hand and that he'd raised his voice too much, so he was apologizing for that."

"That's not fair." Sharon wasn't hungry, but she nibbled at her ham sandwich. It was something to do.

"He still hangs over me in class. Just waiting for the wrong move. Think quick."

Suddenly, the glass eye slid across the table toward her. Sharon dropped her sandwich and grabbed it before it reached the edge. It was surprisingly heavy. The front looked like an eyeball, but there was a hole at the back. "You'd think they'd draw some bloodshot lines in the white part."

"Yeah, right." Richard grinned. "Okay, now put your arms out along the edge of the table, like this." He placed

his arms along his side of the table so they provided a bar-
rier. Sharon copied him and hunched down to munch
her sandwich out of her table-level hand. "Good," he said.
He reached into a pocket and brought out several aggies
and cat's-eye marbles. "Okay, you get the aggies and I get
the little guys."

Richard set the glass eye in the middle of the table.
Then they made up some rules about shooting around it
and began the game. The space was so small, it was next
to impossible to miss, but the rolling, clicking sounds
were comforting.

"My grandmother used to tell me stories," Richard
said, watching an aggie roll toward him. "There was this
one about the *wehtiko*. Ever heard of it?"

"Uh-uh," said Sharon, concentrating on an aggie.

"It's like a cannibal—eats other people. A man-eater."

"A man-eater?"

"There are people around who are sort of like that.
They go after the spirit. Ludlow's one of them—a spirit-
eater. There's always someone waiting to get at part of you,
tear it out and take it away." His hand closed around the
glass eye, and he held it up for a moment between them.
"This is what they give you." With his free hand, he traced
the lower edge of the empty socket. "This is what they take
away."

Sharon couldn't look at him. She watched the cat's-
eye roll toward her.

"When I first saw you, by the garbage pail?" His voice
went up at the end, as if he was asking her a question.

"Yeah?"

"Well, that's what I thought about you—that a spirit-
eater had gotten at you."

It was happening—the Black Hole bit. It was happening right here in the cafeteria, and she'd pushed her hair way back so she couldn't hide behind it.

Then, it faded. Sharon took a deep breath. For the first time, she had managed to fight her way out of the mess inside her head.

"Something the matter?" Richard asked.

"No."

He shrugged. "It's just what I thought that first time I saw you."

The warning bell rang for classes. Richard reached into his pocket and brought out her retainer. As she took it from him, she didn't want to leave, step out of this conversation. "Are you . . . going to be here tomorrow? If a spirit-eater doesn't get you, I mean?"

"It's a date." Richard put his eye back in.

Sharon giggled. "It's got a bit of mustard on it—right over the middle."

He took it out again, licked it, then rubbed it against his T-shirt. "Sloppy eater, eh?"

Chapter 17

Sharon dawdled, kicking chunks of ice. Edmonton skies got dark early; 4:30 P.M. in December already felt like evening. A headache had picked all the sore parts of her brain to pound away at—she'd been kept after school for extra work on her math and it'd worn her out.

Who cares about geometry? Sharon thought. If only I could go home, push open the door, and see Mom sitting there with a smile on her face—a real one, not a fake one. We could sit down, eat some cookies, and talk. If only we could talk for a while, like I do with Richard.

They'd been eating their lunches together for almost two weeks now. Lunch break was her favorite time of the day, separate from the rest of it, like a dream.

She turned and walked up the driveway to Uncle Bert's side door. There was someone sitting on the side entrance stairs—someone wearing rubber boots. Sharon stopped. She could hear Fern humming softly.

"Hi," Sharon said awkwardly.

"Hi." Fern gave a gulping sigh. "I was waiting for you. I knew you had to do extra math after school."

"Well, why didn't you call or something?"

Fern's eyes drifted away like the snow. "I dunno. I just

wanted to wait here, I guess. You're such a secret, Sharon. You keep everything such a big secret."

Sharon sat down next to Fern on the step. It felt good having a person sitting next to her instead of just more air and wind.

"I wrote this poem." Fern opened her duotang and handed her a piece of paper. "You can read it now if you want."

Cautiously, Sharon spread out the paper fluttering in her hand. The poem was titled "Negative Integers."

Life is like a graph,
full of negatives and positives
but it's not a bell curve.
The moon shines on the sadness
in the eyes of all the negative people.
They have no mouths because
no one listens to them.
They are the negative integers.
They might be bag ladies.
They might be lawyers and professors.
They might be the kids who
sit next to you and wonder
if you will remember them, ever,
when they turn the corner and are gone.

Sharon swallowed. "It's good," she whispered.

Fern's mitten touched Sharon's arm gently, once. "I found out my mom's having an affair," she said. "One day when I came home from school, this guy was there. He's an anthropologist." She was quiet for a while. "The Anthropologist," she repeated with distaste.

Sharon looked at her. "Why didn't you tell me?"

"It's not something you want to advertise," Fern muttered. "Dad's away a lot, being a lawyer. He's always going to different cities. He's probably having an affair, too. They're always arguing—yelling." Fern stopped and stared off, sucking in her lower lip. Then she was blinking hard.

"I didn't tell anyone," she said softly. "My mom? She asked me not to tell Dad. I guess she thinks Dad doesn't love her." Fern's voice trailed off, then came back. "Maybe he doesn't anymore." She wiped her eyes, then put her chin on her knees. "My brother's always off playing basketball or volleyball. Or he's practicing his stupid trumpet and telling me to get out of the room. So I couldn't talk to him about it." She glanced at Sharon. "What . . . d'you do without a dad? What's it like?"

Sharon shrugged. "What's it like with a dad?"

Fern gave a small laugh. "Yeah, I guess."

"D'you think your parents are going to split up?"

"I think they hate each other's guts," Fern said softly. "Sometimes they hate each other so much, it kind of floats around the house like poison gas."

"Your mom's okay," Sharon said dubiously. "Is your dad?"

Beside her, Fern exploded. "They're both okay . . . when they're not around each other, that is. They don't, like, hit each other. They just yell all the time. All the time."

She paused and smiled wistfully. "I remember one time, I was around eight and Dad wanted to make everyone a milkshake. Mom said she'd do it, but Dad was really into it, so she just sat there and watched. She was smiling. She used to smile about him a lot, and he was whistling 'The Pink Panther' and wearing an apron. Just before he turned the blender on, Mom's smile got *huge*. The stuff shot up and plastered all over the ceiling. He forgot to put the lid on it."

Sharon giggled and Fern flashed a grin. "Mom laughed so hard she was screaming. She was on the floor, rolling around. Dad stared at the ceiling for a while. Then he got down on the floor, too, and tickled Mom until she was begging him to stop. That's the way they used to be." There was another pause.

"Living with my mom and my Uncle Bert," Sharon began, then stopped, her eyes suddenly stinging. "My mom's mostly tired. Sometimes, I think when I come home from school . . . she'll be gone."

She hadn't ever thought this in words before. But she had felt it every time she'd dragged her feet up the driveway to Uncle Bert's door.

"What d'you mean?" Fern asked.

"I dunno. Sometimes I just think . . . she might not be here anymore."

Fern started to move one boot around in the snow. "What's your Uncle Bert like?"

"He's like . . ." Sharon couldn't think of a description. About her, the snow lifted and fell, like wings—angel wings. "He's like the Angel Gabriel, always announcing the end of the world."

"Huh?" asked Fern.

"Or Moses giving out the commandments. The Old Testament, y'know?"

"What's that?" asked Fern.

"The Bible," said Sharon.

Fern shrugged. "Never read it. So, he's biblical, your Uncle Bert?"

"Biblical, for sure," Sharon grinned. "That's it. Ever biblical, my Uncle Bert."

Fern snickered. Sharon leaned back against the door. A smile glowed throughout her body, then faded out.

"It'd be nice to want to come home," Sharon said slowly, "sometime."

"Yeah." Fern sighed and stood up. "You changed your hair, eh? Pushed it back? Looks good."

"Yeah?"

"Well, I'd better go. I'm sorry . . . about Home Ec. and the detention and all. I guess I was just pissed off about my parents."

"But what's that got to do with Home Ec.?" Sharon asked.

Fern shrugged. "Ms. Bohn pisses me off, too. Sometimes the whole world pisses me off."

"Oh," said Sharon. "Well, why get a detention over it?"

"You burned those cookies," Fern pointed out.

"Yeah." Sharon grinned. "It was . . . biblical, eh?"

"Yeah." Fern laughed. "Good hair, Sharon—keep the face."

Fern walked backward down the driveway, waved, then half-skipped, half-ran out of sight. Sharon stood for a while, her hand on the doorknob. It was funny—the way she hadn't put words to the way she felt about her mother, about Uncle Bert, about getting mad, until she'd talked to Fern. It was funny how putting the words to it made her feel better because it hadn't changed anything, really.

She turned the door handle. "Into the Old Testament," she muttered and walked in.

Chapter 18

The following day, Richard wasn't in his usual seat in the cafeteria. Sharon and Fern found a place in the crowd and began to explore their bag lunches. Fern placed her gum on the end of her right index finger for safekeeping while she drank her chocolate milk. Then she seemed to forget about it and waved it all over the place as she talked.

Sharon was watching the gum on the end of Fern's finger, hoping it wouldn't fly off. With her luck, it'd land in the middle of her hair and get stuck. She'd end up having to get an intense haircut, probably a crew cut. Sharon focused on the wad of gum.

Suddenly, Fern stood up, waving her arms. "Over here! Hey—Richard!"

Sharon twisted around on the bench so quickly that one of her feet got caught around a table leg. Richard was over by the door. He saw Fern waving and walked toward them, his face expressionless.

Sharon gulped. A moment ago, while Fern was talking, Sharon had been thinking about Richard's face, the two smile lines on the left side of his mouth. Now her heart was pounding blood through her entire body. She'd eaten lunch with him for almost two weeks. This had never happened before. Why now? The bench wobbled as he slid in beside her and dropped a brown bag lunch onto the table. He flicked a hand against hers. "Hi, Sharon."

"Hi," she managed.

"Hey," said Fern. "How's it going with Ludlow?"

Richard's hand tensed but his voice was steady. "All right, I guess. Mostly, he's leaving me alone."

"Well, maybe it did some good then," said Fern.

Richard's hand hovered over Sharon's retainer. She had been keeping it in full view, away from Fern's good intentions. Slowly, he placed his glass eye on top of it. Sharon grinned.

"Uh . . ." Fern gulped.

"Yes?" drawled Richard.

"Uh . . ." repeated Fern, "that's kind of gross, when we're eating, y'know?"

"I just wanted to keep an eye on Sharon's retainer," he said.

Laughter ballooned in Sharon's stomach. He grinned at her, his two smile lines deepening. Whatever she'd been afraid of when he'd walked in was suddenly gone.

"Biblical!" said Fern. "I've got an idea."

Richard's smile faded. "Yeah?"

"Well, this morning, we found out we have to do a presentation for Social Studies. Sharon and I signed up to do this one about the Plains Indians."

"So?" Richard started pushing holes into his sandwich. Peanut butter mushed out the sides.

"Well, Alberta's the Plains, isn't it? Flat enough. I was just thinking—why don't we interview you?"

Richard's hand jerked.

"What're you talking about?" Sharon asked.

Fern blinked rapidly, her cheeks flushing, but she kept

going. "Well, I think it's dumb to read those textbooks again. What do we need to know more about tepees and hunting buffalo? They make it sound like Saturday morning cartoons."

"Thanks a lot," said Richard.

"No, I don't mean your history is . . . boring or anything," Fern stumbled. "I mean, if we want to know about what it's like to be an Indian, why don't we ask you?"

The center of Richard's sandwich was very flat.

"I don't know if I'd want to do that," Sharon said slowly. "I mean, if there was something different about me . . ." She stopped, feeling herself go hot. "When I had to give that presentation about the paper dolls, I didn't want to."

"I heard about that," Richard said.

Sharon's face turned itself toward the wall. "You did?"

"Ah—who cares about hobbies?" Richard said.

Her eyes wandered back to her lunch. "Yeah, who cares?" She started poking her sandwich, too, but it was made of tuna. The goop fell onto the table and made a mess.

"Would you rather we kept reading the same old stuff?" said Fern.

"The same old stuff," Richard echoed. "You know what the real stuff is?"

"No," said Fern.

"Your teacher wouldn't let me say it," said Richard. "I'd tell them things she wouldn't believe."

"So, we just won't tell Ms. Okashimo what we're going to do," said Fern. "We just open the door, and you walk in, and we run the interview."

"You asking me to skip class?" asked Richard. "Ludlow's class? He's my L.A. teacher."

"Oh," hesitated Fern.

Oh dear, Sharon thought.

Richard was ripping the flattened sandwich into small strips. "Ah, what the hell. Wouldn't be the first time."

"But you've got to be honest," said Fern. "And we've got to run this like professionals, right? I'll interview you."

"What's Sharon going to do?" Richard demanded.

Nothing, thought Sharon. Sit at the back of the class and watch.

Thoughtfully, Fern poked her gum back into her mouth. "Well, why don't you be the opposition?"

"Huh?" asked Sharon.

"Why don't you be someone who's racist?" Fern suggested.

"Someone who hates me," Richard grinned.

In her head, Sharon saw her Uncle Bert's mouth moving. "Dirty bastards—they're all drunks. Got lice." She knew, somehow, that Fern had never heard anyone talk like her Uncle Bert. Suddenly, Sharon wanted to show Fern, show Ms. Okashimo, show the whole world her Uncle Bert. Even if it meant standing in front of the class to do it. She nodded. "Okay."

"This is great!" Fern exclaimed. "It's due the first day after Christmas break. We should start working on the interview questions." She ripped a piece of paper out of her duotang.

Richard rolled the thinned sandwich up into some waxed paper and stuffed it back into his bag. "Let's get at it."

Chapter 19

School let out for the holidays on the twenty-third of December. Eleven days alone stretched out ahead of Sharon. Fern and her family had gone to Banff for a ski trip. Richard hadn't said what he'd be doing. Sharon figured she'd spend a lot of time at the library.

"What would you like for Christmas—a new set of paper dolls?" her mother asked on the twenty-fourth.

"I don't play with paper dolls much anymore," Sharon replied. "They have mostly a nostalgic purpose, these days."

A smile glimmered around her mother's mouth. "Nostalgia, eh? Well, how about some fancy barrettes for your hair?"

Sharon poked at her potato salad, felt the flush prickle across her face. "Maybe nothing too fancy. Nothing neon."

Her mother reached over and rumpled her hair. "Nothing that'll make anyone notice you, eh? My beautiful daughter."

Sharon's flush was now a deep red.

"Eat your salad," smiled her mother. "Put some meat on those bones."

Christmas Eve was quiet. They watched a TV special and then Sharon wrapped gifts in her room—bubble bath for her mother, a large bowl for Uncle Bert. It had Edmonton Oilers hockey figures skating around the outside. It was his favorite team. In the morning, he tore the paper off like a little boy, then stared at the bowl as if he'd never seen one before.

"It's for popcorn," Sharon muttered. "While you watch TV."

"Oh." Uncle Bert sounded surprised. After a pause, he cleared his throat and said, "Thanks, Sharon."

When her mother unwrapped the bubble bath, a quick smile came and went on her face. Sharon knew her mother was thinking of the time before they'd moved in with Uncle Lawrence. She could remember the long baths her mother had taken then, the white bubbles a soft cloud, the scent of lilacs on her skin for the rest of the evening.

Uncle Bert kept staring at his bowl. Sharon opened packages of barrettes, socks and underwear, a new blouse and sweater, slippers and a copy of *Two Moons In August* by Martha Brooks. "Thanks, Mom."

"And Uncle Bert," her mother said.

"Thanks, Uncle Bert." Sharon's eyes skipped over his face.

He grunted. Sharon spent the early afternoon in her room, arranging and rearranging the barrettes in her hair. One pair was peach with small blue flowers, the other a deep red. She turned her head this way and that, her eyes traveling around the outside of her reflection. It was hard to look at herself. Sharon closed her eyes, concentrated, then opened them. There was a quick impression of dark brown eyes, a slightly open mouth, and fluffy brown hair pinned back by red barrettes.

Her eyes flicked away, then back. Her hair had never seemed fluffy before. And it looked like it might have coppery streaks in it. She fingered a strand and slid another glance across her reflection. She looked okay . . . maybe. Maybe she was even a little pretty. Maybe, if she practiced, she'd get used to the barrettes enough to be able to wear them to school after the holidays.

The next time he saw her, Uncle Bert noticed. "Well, that looks okay, kid," he said. He was sitting in front of the TV, eating popcorn out of his Edmonton Oilers bowl.

Sharon took this as a compliment. She had been watching her uncle, noting the way he sat, what he said. He kept up a running commentary on politicians, bad drivers, and the neighbor's dog, but it was a while before he got around to Indians again. The supper dishes had been finished. Uncle Bert sat in the dining room watching the news. From the kitchen table, Sharon could hear a journalist begin a report on the progress of the Lubicon land claims issue in northern Alberta.

"Whiners!" Uncle Bert hollered. "Lousy wagon-burners!"

If she was going to represent her uncle, she needed to add to her collection of one-liners. She couldn't keep yelling, "Get the buggers!" for twenty minutes. Sharon checked her barrettes to make sure they were in place.

"Uncle Bert?"

He shifted on the sofa, not looking at her. "Uh?"

"I was wondering if I could get your opinion?"

There was a pause. "What about?"

"Well . . ." Sharon hesitated. "About land claims and Indians and stuff?"

Uncle Bert grunted again. "Bunch of drunken bastards," he muttered. "Want what doesn't belong to them.

Should've shot them all when we took over this country. Wouldn't be having the problems we've got now." His voice became louder. "It's Oka all over the country. Indians think they own the universe. They think they own my store and my house."

His face twisted. "'We were here first.' Well, who's here *now!* Next thing, they'll want us to be paying taxes to the moose and the buffalo . . . to the amoeba! The amoeba were here before all of us, weren't they?"

Sharon tried another question. "So you think Oka was because the mayor wanted to expand a golf course?"

"A man wanted to pay good money for land nobody was doing nuthin' with, Sharon. Just a place to play a little golf and relax. Mohawks whining about sacred land. They're savages and criminals. Shot a police officer."

Sharon hesitated. "But there were bullet holes in the trees behind the Mohawks at shoulder height."

Uncle Bert was still staring at the TV, but now his neck muscles went rigid. "Bullshit!"

Sharon heard her mother's worried sigh. Uncle Bert's voice subsided to a mumble. "Turn the whole goddam reserve into a golf course—that's what I say. Turn every reserve into a golf course. That'd be a good use of natural resources."

Sharon decided she had enough material. She climbed the stairs quietly. She passed her bedroom mirror, intending to flop down on the bed and practice her lines. Then she stopped and turned.

For the past two days, she'd been giving herself quick over-the-shoulder glances in the mirror as she walked by. Tomorrow, school started again. Her whole class would be staring at her for twenty minutes. Slowly, she approached the mirror.

There was that pale, slim face, the dark brown eyes. The mouth seemed large, oversized to her. A brief picture of Uncle Bert's lips twisting around the word, "Bullshit!" flashed through her head. Was that what her mouth looked like?

"No," she whispered to the face in the mirror. This would be her New Year's resolution, three days late. "I'm not like Uncle Bert. He's not my real family. He doesn't belong to me."

There was her fluffy, brown hair, streaked copper. Uncle Bert was bald. Sharon touched her hair and smiled.

Chapter 20

Sharon watched the classroom clock wind its way through the half-year between 9:00 and 9:30 A.M. So far, the morning had been very stressful, kids staring at her barrettes, teachers giving her compliments. Fern kept turning in her seat to send her encouraging glances. She'd been at Sharon's side door at 8:20, had burst into a delighted grin when Sharon shuffled out.

"Gorgeous!" she'd said.

Sharon had her doubts. She could see an awful lot of the world going on around her now—more of the walls, the doors, the ever-shifting and fidgeting kids. There was so much of it, so much to keep her eyes on.

At 9:30, there was a knock at the door. Fern shot Sharon a bright blue stare and was up out of her desk. Giant, invisible hands lifted Sharon out of her seat and pushed her along the aisle after Fern so closely that she bumped into her at the door.

"Where are you ladies going?" Ms. Okashimo called.

Fern pulled open the door. Richard leaned in the doorway, his dark gaze jumping from Fern to Sharon. Ms. Okashimo came up behind them.

"Richard's helping us with our presentation," Fern said.

Richard was still looking at Sharon. She could feel his gaze move over her hair, forehead, eyes. She looked away to Ms. Okashimo.

"He's part of our project," she stammered. "We're going to interview him."

"Does your teacher know you're here?" Ms. Okashimo asked.

"Sure." Richard kept looking at Sharon, a question-mark smile on his face.

"We wanted it to be a surprise," Fern added.

Ms. Okashimo paused. "Let me send a note to your teacher while you set up."

"All right!" said Fern.

Ms. Okashimo sent Frank off with a message for Mr. Ludlow while Fern dragged chairs to the front of the class. Sharon stood with Richard, watching the class put away books and settle down.

"Your hair looks really nice," Richard said in a low voice.

"So does yours." One of her hands came up and fiddled with a strand of hair. They looked at each other, strange, shy smiles sliding over their mouths.

"C'mon, you guys," said Fern. "I got the chairs set up. What're you doing?"

"Nuthin'." Sharon's and Richard's voices overlapped.

Fern's grin knew too much. "Yeah, right."

Standing in front of the class ended up being easier than Sharon had thought. No one paid any attention to her. Every eye settled on Richard as he leaned against the back of a chair and met the gaze of each kid, one by one. For the first time, Sharon really looked at him. She saw the black sweatshirt, the sleeves that were a little too short, the well-worn jeans. She saw how dark his skin and hair were, how the one glass eye sat oddly still while the other challenged. She moved over, stood closer so their shoulders almost touched.

Frank returned with Mr. Ludlow's reply. For a moment, Ms. Okashimo frowned down at it, then smiled at them and walked to the back of the room. "Well, class, Sharon and Fern are doing their presentation today. They've asked another student to participate. We want to welcome Richard Calliou to our class. Thank you for joining us, Richard."

Richard nodded stiffly, his gaze on the opposite wall. Then they sat down, Richard in the middle, the three of them perched nervously on the edge of a new year.

Chapter 21

Fern took a minute to stare down at the toes of her runners. Then she looked up. "When I think about the first peoples of Canada, what do I think about? I remember pictures of Oka, pictures of soldiers with guns pointed at Indian people. I remember the protests about logging in Clayoquot Sound. I keep hearing about culture and what a difference it makes when you don't have your own culture. Well, Sharon Frejer and I were born in Canada, and so was Richard Calliou, but life has been very different for him." She paused. "So we thought we'd ask him about it."

Richard had turned his head to look at Fern. One eyebrow raised, he was smiling slightly. Otherwise, he remained slouched in his chair, arms crossed.

Fern took up an official interviewer's position. "Hello, Richard Calliou. How are you?"

He grinned. "Fine—anything to get out of class, y'know."

The class laughed. Sharon's muscles shook with relief.

"On the other side of Richard Calliou, we have Sharon Frejer, Executive Director of the White Minority Association. Sharon believes we should cut off all Indian rights, take away their land, and stop paying welfare to them."

Sharon stuck her eyes to Fern's face. "I think we should turn all reserves into golf courses," she said. "That way we'd get more money out of them. I think that'd be a good use of natural resources."

"Well," said Fern, "as you can see, we have different opinions on our panel of experts. Why don't we start by hearing what some of your life has been like, Richard?"

"Sure," Richard shrugged.

"Where were you born?"

"Edmonton."

"Were you born in a hospital, just like everyone else?" asked Sharon, listening to Uncle Bert in her head.

"I think so," grinned Richard. "I can't remember that far back."

Sharon waited for the class to stop laughing. "At tax-payers' expense," she said. "We paid for that."

"Well, I don't think I could've waited inside until my mother had more money," Richard observed.

"What happened after you were born?" Fern asked. "How'd you end up here?"

"I was the sixth kid in my family. I grew up on the Sucker Creek Reserve. My dad died in a car crash when I was about two. I don't remember him. I had cancer when I was three, and that's when they cut off my leg and took out my eye. I was in the hospital for a while." He grinned at Sharon. "Yeah, taxpayers paid for it."

"Doesn't your mother work for a living?" she asked disapprovingly.

"I didn't know her much either. She died of TB when I was three."

Sharon glanced quickly at Fern and saw her eyes

looking back, slightly scared. They hadn't known all the answers to the questions they'd set up with Richard.

Richard cleared his throat. "When I didn't have parents left, I lived with my grandmother until she died. Then I was seven. The government put me in a receiving home in Grande Prairie for a while."

"What's that?" Fern had lost her official voice.

"You're just there for a while, until they decide what they're really going to do with you," Richard said.

"What was it like?" asked Fern.

"It's like a group home, but the kids don't stay as long—maybe three weeks, so it's pretty crazy. You don't really get to know anyone. When you're seven, you don't know what the hell's happening to you. You just hide out in your room, watching the big white people walk around and tell you what to do."

"Okay," said Fern. "What happened next?"

"Foster homes," said Richard. "Some on farms. All white people. One family was really good to me, treated me like their own kids. I didn't want to leave there. Lots of families take in foster kids for the money. One place gave me leftovers for supper, kept calling me a stinking bastard." He paused. "Some of them beat you up. One guy used to come after me with a baseball bat.

"I have this one older brother, Matt. We talk on the phone. He visits when he can, but that can be hard. See, every time they move you to a different place, they change your school. I went through four schools one year. It gets to the point where the social worker drops you off at another house and you don't even unpack your suitcase. Even at the good places, you don't unpack your suitcase."

"That's crazy!" said Fern.

Sharon felt as if she was supposed to say something at this point. "How come they keep moving you around? Were you doing something wrong?"

"That's okay," said Richard, turning to look at her. "I know you're supposed to hate me. You ever heard of Richard Cardinal?"

The class was silent. Ms. Okashimo spoke for the first time from the back of the room. "That was very sad."

"They moved him around a lot, and he hung himself," said Richard. "Seventeen years old and he'd lived in sixteen foster families already. I can relate. It happened here in Alberta. 'Richard Cardinal, Richard Cardinal'— that's what the kids used to call me at one school, just for a joke."

Silence filled Sharon's mouth, her head. She stared at him.

"They're always flipping social workers on you," he continued. "I don't even bother remembering their names anymore. I used to call them up, but they never remember me without looking me up on some computer first."

"Social workers are overworked," Sharon stammered.

"My last foster home was the place that guy came at me with a baseball bat. I set a fire in their basement. After that, I got stuck in the Youth Detention Center, and when I did my time there, they moved me to the Youth Center where I am now."

"What happened to the guy with the baseball bat?" asked Fern.

"Nuthin'," said Richard. "He's probably using it on his own kids."

Fern had forgotten her questions. She sat and stared at Richard.

You are Uncle Bert, Sharon had to remind herself. She

leaned forward. "Indian kids got an attitude problem," she said loudly. "Maybe a baseball bat is too much, but there must've been something that set him off. Indians can't take orders—can't accept when someone else is in charge."

The stares of the class were on her now. They had forgotten she was acting. She pulled on Uncle Bert's face. "You're lucky to be alive at all," she continued. She made the words hard and loud. "I don't get all this complaining about traditional values. The Chinks and Pakis keep their traditional values at home. They work for a living and fit in fine."

"What d'you think about that?" Fern asked hastily, cutting her off.

Richard winked at Sharon. She pretended to ignore him. You wanted to know what my Uncle Bert was like, Sharon thought silently, looking at Fern.

"How does it feel to be an Indian?" Fern continued.

Richard looked her square in the eye. "It feels good to be Cree. How does it feel to be white?"

Fern's eyes widened. "Sometimes, not so good."

Richard's face tensed and he swallowed. "There was a time when I hated being Cree. The only time I felt half okay about my skin was in the summer, when everyone else was trying to get a tan and look like me. All the Indians I used to see were asking for money or in group homes."

Richard paused. Sharon heard him pull air in suddenly, saw his shoulders shake with the effort. He doesn't want to cry, she thought, and he thinks he's going to.

"Once, they even put me in a hospital psych ward to check out my head, see if I was a nut case. See, I won't just shut up and take it like a good little prairie nigger. I'm not appropriate."

He stopped, then continued. "How many of you ever been in a group home?" No hands went up. Richard nodded. "About half the kids I see in group homes are Cree or Métis, and none of the staff are. It's not that I don't like them. They're okay. But it's sort of like . . ." He grinned suddenly. "It's like waking up one morning and everyone around you is a girl. You're the only guy. And there's no guys' can. There's no clothes for guys in stores. There's no football or hockey. It's just all gone." He snapped his fingers. "Like that."

Boys were grimacing, trying to laugh. Richard waited them out.

"Except it's more important than clothes or football or hockey. It's everything. It's everything around you. You're dropped into a place where nuthin' is like you. Nuthin'. No matter how long you hang around. So you end up feeling like nuthin', too. I'm mad. Not crazy. Mad. I wouldn't be white for anything. I'm Cree and I'm gonna make good just like a Cree."

Sharon swallowed hard. She remembered all the lines she'd been planning to say, but Uncle Bert didn't belong here and she cut him off.

"Well, what d'you think it means to be Cree?" asked Fern.

Richard paused, staring off. "Cree is what my brother Matt is. It's not something you can say in words. It's the way you are. You don't really talk about it much. That's the main difference I see in whites—all this talk, talk, talk about everything, but nothing changes. They talk so they don't have to change.

"My grandmother told me stories about our people. Then I come to school and learn the Indians were running around after the buffalo until Columbus showed up and straightened them all out. See, when you hear stuff like that and you know it's shit, then you got to wonder if all the rest of the stuff in school is shit, too. Why bother learning lies?"

Some of the kids were turning around and looking at Ms. Okashimo. She nodded calmly at them.

"Like, when you think Indian, you think feathers and weird singing, right?" Richard asked.

Some of the kids were grinning at each other.

"Well, get used to the singing because you're gonna hear a lot more of it," said Richard. "But now you can add Ovide Mercredi to the picture, too."

There was a pause. Ms. Okashimo added, "And I'm sure we'll think of Richard Calliou, too."

Someone started clapping and the rest of the students joined in. Richard stared at the floor, face tight. Sharon hunched on her chair, hoping he could beat the need to cry.

"Guess I took over your interview," he said to Fern.

"That's good," she shrugged.

"Heil Hitler," he saluted Sharon.

"But I had to," she protested.

"I know," he assured her. Standing, he turned toward the door. "Well, it's back to class."

"Thanks, Richard," said Ms. Okashimo. "Mr. Ludlow knows you'll be on your way back about now."

"He'll like that," said Richard. He glanced at Sharon and grinned. The door closed behind him.

Sharon dropped down into her desk. It was over. Richard had made it through, and so had she. If she could do this, she could do anything.

Chapter 22

"What team are you on for Color Night?" Frank Giles asked.

It was the week following the interview. They were sitting on the 7 Eleven parking lot cement bumpers, about to devour some muffins Fern had brought to school. That morning, the home room teachers had begun their campaign to get everyone involved in a February sports event called Color Night. The school had been divided into four teams: green, gold, blue, and red.

"Our class is on the Gold Team," Fern said.

"We're on Blue," said Richard. "You in anything?"

"Yeah, I'm on the volleyball team." Fern was chewing her gum with a frantic energy, trying to keep warm.

"You in anything, Sharon?" Richard asked.

Frank snorted.

Flushing, Sharon poked at the snow with a stick. "Uh . . . actually . . . as a matter of fact . . . not really, I guess."

Fern giggled. "She won't even join the audience."

"I'll make you a dare," Richard said.

"Do we have to?" Sharon asked.

Richard grinned. "My part's harder."

This was of little comfort to Sharon.

"I'll enter the long foot race—the one all the way around the gym." Richard's voice seemed to be teasing her, but Sharon could hear a good deal of purpose in it. "Actually, as a matter of fact, I guess I already signed up."

Before she could stop herself, Sharon's eyes had darted toward his false leg.

"Hey, man," Frank stammered. "How're you gonna . . . ? You can't . . ."

"I can," said Richard.

Surprise brushed over Sharon. It was true. Nothing was stopping him.

"So you pick something," Richard continued.

But I can't, she thought, and poked at the snow with her stick.

"Why d'you want to do this?" Fern asked. "Like, with your leg and all, won't it . . . ?"

Richard whacked his false leg. "I just want to, so I'm going to. Hey—want to see it?" Without waiting for an answer, he slid his sweat pants up over the knee. Sharon stared at the heavy, beige leg, the sudden change to warm, brown skin above the knee.

"It's held on by a vacuum," Richard explained. "You just slide this to one side. The vacuum is released and the leg comes off." He demonstrated, pushing a panel at the top to one side, and the false limb came off. Sharon got a quick glance of the stump. Then Richard slid the tight-fitting section at the top of the false limb back on and closed the panel again. He pulled down the leg of his sweats. "See? Easy on, easy off," he grinned. "Let's see you do that."

The three of them stared at him for a moment. Then Frank pulled off his baseball cap and twirled it on a finger. "I can do it with my cap."

Richard grinned happily. Then he leaned toward Sharon. "Color Night, Sharon. Think of something."

Frank stretched and stood up. A lot of kids still made Paper Doll Queen jokes about Sharon, but Frank had stopped. He shoved Richard playfully. "Gotta go shoot baskets. We'll crush you Blue losers."

As Frank headed off, Richard shifted and put his arm around Sharon's shoulders. Her heart jumped about two feet. She shot a quick glance at Fern, who snapped a bubble she'd been working on, as if nothing earth shattering, nothing completely out of this world had happened. Richard hummed softly and looked across the street. Once her heart had climbed back down to where it was supposed to be, Sharon found his arm very comfortable.

Fern opened the bag of muffins and passed them each one. Quickly, Richard finished his first and reached for another.

"Sharon," Fern said, "you haven't even started yours. Something wrong with my cooking?"

"No." Sharon was thinking about Richard's arm around her shoulder. "They're good."

"You never eat." Fern stood up, another muffin in her hand. "That's why you're so thin."

"I eat."

"No, you don't. You always play with your food." Laughing, Fern aimed the muffin straight for Sharon's mouth. "Open wide."

Sharon opened her mouth to protest, and the muffin made its way in, pushing against her teeth and tongue. It crumbled, pushed against her nose. Suddenly, she couldn't breathe. A scream was rising in her throat, but she couldn't get it out. Then she heard Uncle Lawrence's voice.

"You think you're gonna sit at my table and not eat

what's put in front of you? This is the rule, kid: You goddam eat the food or this is what happens."

It wasn't a muffin anymore, and it wasn't an Edmonton parking lot. It was Rockwood and there were mashed
potatoes all over her face, pushed into her nose, meat loaf
caught in her throat, Uncle Lawrence's hand cramming
more and more in. She couldn't swallow. She began to
choke, was trying to pull away, but he had his hand on the
back of her neck, keeping her head in place. More and
more was rammed down her throat.

Then the winter wind came back and she was leaning against Richard, sucking in air, trying to get as much
as possible. Her head hurt. The muffin lay in broken
pieces all over her coat and lap.

"Sharon?" Fern was crouched in front of her.

"Not so close," Sharon gasped.

"I'm sorry," Fern whispered.

Now she could see them again. Ducking her head,
Sharon began to pick muffin pieces off her coat. "Sorry,"
she mumbled. "I'm all right now."

"What were you thinking about?" Richard's voice was
gentle.

"My Uncle Lawrence." Sharon stopped, afraid the
memory would take shape and shove itself at her again.

"Your Uncle Lawrence from Rockwood?" Fern unfold-
ed herself from a nervous ball.

"Yeah."

"And . . . ?" Richard was still waiting.

"Sometimes . . ." Sharon started, then stopped. She'd
never talked about this to anyone. Just the thought of
putting words to it made her head feel dizzy and dark.
But Richard had managed to talk about his life in front
of the whole class.

"Sometimes," she started again, staring down, "if I didn't eat, my Uncle Lawrence made me. Like that."

"What?" Fern's voice was soft.

"Sharon?" Richard's hand was shifting in and out of the hair on her shoulder.

"Yeah?"

"That happens to me, too, sometimes."

"What?"

"As if something from before is happening now."

"Yeah?" She could look at him now.

"Yeah." He touched her cheek. "Ludlow can make me feel that way."

"I'm sorry," Fern said. "I'll never be your Uncle Lawrence again, I promise."

The bell rang. Richard pushed himself to his feet and stood looming over Sharon. "Come with me now," he said in his Frankenstein voice. "We are going to sign you up for Color Night."

"But I don't want to," said Sharon weakly.

Richard grabbed her hand and pulled her to her feet. "You can race me around the gym. You'll beat me."

Chapter 23

Sharon stood in a line about to rotate onto the volleyball court. She watched Fern throw herself through the air after the ball. Someone flubbed up. A math teacher, who was the referee, blew the whistle and everyone rotated. Richard stepped onto the court. She was next.

Not only had Richard signed her up for the Color Night bean-bag toss, but he'd gotten a sudden urge to play noon hour volleyball and signed all three of them up for one team. Sweat trickled down from Sharon's armpits. The teacher wrapped his lips around the whistle, ready to blow, when the PA system came on. "Would Mr. Abercrombie please come to the office? Mr. Abercrombie, please come to the office immediately."

Mr. Abercrombie scratched his crew cut, then focused on Fern and tossed her the whistle. "Take over for me. I'll be back as soon as I can."

Fern stepped up on the chair, swinging the whistle around her neck with a pleased look. "Everyone ready?" She blew the whistle.

The ball bounced from one pair of hands to another. Richard jumped up to spike a serve and sent it back over but stumbled and half-fell as he came down. Sharon flinched, but he balanced himself, twisting to watch the ball. The whistle shrieked again.

"Sharon—that's you." Fern was grinning down at her.

"I know." Sharon stepped gingerly onto the court.

"You'll do great," Richard laughed.

The whistle shrieked again. Fern liked being loud. The ball flew over the net, right above Sharon's head. Everyone was shifting on their feet, turning to see the ball, their runners squeaking on the floor. Richard stepped forward and bumped the ball with his forearms, but it veered off into the watching crowd. Sharon winced. Richard just shrugged and faced the net again. Fern blew her whistle.

"Loser!" someone yelled from the sidelines.

"He's just a one-eyed prairie nigger," someone else hooted.

Sharon looked toward the voices. Some of the kids watching the game were laughing. Richard stared straight ahead at the net, his face rigid. "Ignore it," he said, without looking at her. "They're in my class."

"Why don't you go back to your tepee?" the first voice yelled.

Now she could tell who they were—two boys standing over by the wall. Nearby girls were laughing at their jokes.

"Hey!" yelled Fern. "You want to be racist, go do it somewhere else."

"Yeah," someone on the other team agreed loudly and tossed Fern the ball. It was Len Razlaff. "Can it, you guys."

Fern turned to throw the ball to the server.

"She must be the one going out with the Indian," one of the boys said loudly, ignoring Len. "That's why she's sticking up for him. It's Fern—that's your name, right? Hey, Fern, talk to us, Indian-lover."

Richard was opening and closing his hands, flexing the fingers out wide, closing them in again. An invisible line of panic ran from Richard through Sharon to Fern— it pulsed through them in waves. If one of them blew it here, all three got hurt.

Slowly, Fern turned to face the two boys, still holding the ball. "You're being real ignorant, you know that?"

Sharon realized that no one had noticed her. It was just like she'd wanted. No one knew she was the one going out with Richard, if that was really what she and Richard were doing. Neither Fern nor Richard were likely to point her out.

"Yeah, yeah," said one of the boys. "Can't get a white guy, eh, Fern?"

"Who'd want you?" Fern was going into battle position. Richard hadn't moved.

Slowly, Sharon's feet unstuck themselves from the floor. It was hard to get her legs moving, but she turned and walked around Richard, who still stood staring straight ahead. Now she was walking across the court toward the group of watching kids. They were getting bigger, their eyes starting to focus on her. She kept her eyes up there on the faces of the two boys. Everything was suddenly quiet.

"I'm the one you're talking about," she said. Her voice was a high, tight line, very clear. "What's it to you, anyway?"

Everyone was looking at her in surprise. Then a boy snorted. "Isn't this the one who plays with paper dolls?"

Laughter spread through the crowd, washed over Sharon in a hot flush. She opened her mouth to reply, but the hooting was too loud. Then a volleyball came hurtling through the air and hit the last speaker square in the face. He staggered back, raising a hand to one eye, and bent over. Another ball whizzed by the forehead of the second boy. There was a silence and the whistle shrieked again.

"Anyone else with something stupid to say?" Fern asked. She held a third ball in her hands. Everyone got lockjaw.

Sharon picked up the two balls that were rolling unchecked and turned back. She walked staring at her feet, but then Richard was stepping in front of her, taking the balls from her hands, blocking her path. She had to look up.

The smile that sat on his mouth was working to keep the pain all over his face in check. Around them, kids shifted back into player positions. Richard tossed one ball to the server, the other to Fern. "They're assholes," he said to Sharon softly. "Unless they're putting their fist through your teeth, you ignore them, okay?"

He touched her arm, then moved into his position at net. Fern's whistle blew again, but Sharon heard his next words. "Going out with me, eh?" He was grinning again, his face half-turned toward her.

From her position, Sharon glanced at him, her face at medium heat. "Guess so." She smiled.

Mr. Abercrombie walked up to the net, panting from his quick run back. "Everything all right here?"

Fern handed him the whistle and jumped down. On the sidelines, one of the two boys was still holding a hand over his eye. "Okay," Fern said.

Richard nodded to himself. "Okay," he repeated softly.

Okay, Sharon thought.

Chapter 24

The school halls were full of kids sliding knapsacks onto their shoulders. It was the end of the day, and Sharon was turning the corner toward Richard's locker. A lunch bag flew by her head and split open into moldy sandwiches. At first, Sharon wanted to duck. Then she grinned like everyone else. It was just some kids joking around. No one was after her. Even though her heart was pounding, she didn't want to turn and run. Things had changed since last September.

Richard hadn't been around at lunch, but she could see him shoving books into his locker. Sharon leaned against the next locker and waited for him to look up.

"We missed you at lunch," she said finally.

"Hi." When Richard glanced at her, his face didn't move into its usual smile. He lifted an arm up as if to grab his jacket and let it fall back to his side. Then he stood staring down.

"What's the matter?" Sharon asked.

There was a pause. "Nuthin'." Again, Richard reached for his jacket and let his arm fall back.

"How come you didn't eat lunch with us?"

"Busy."

Sharon's face went hot. "Okay." Not knowing what else to do, she turned to leave.

Richard's hand was on her arm. "Wait. Just wait until everyone's gone."

They stood silently until the hall was empty. Richard spoke without looking at her.

"They're moving me."

Everything went dark for a second, then came back.

"I had a case conference today. They told me they're moving me to a group home in High Level. They say I'll be closer to my brother Matt, and the program there'll be good for me."

"They can't move you!" Sharon was almost shouting.

Richard spoke in a monotone. "I can't do nuthin' about it. They say it's because I'm doing so well. It's a step up."

"Don't you want to stay?"

"Yeah." There was the sudden sound of something caught in his throat. "I'm just getting used to this place."

Sharon sat on the floor. "What's a case conference?"

"It's this meeting, where all these staff get together. There's your social worker and your key staff and the agency head and the nurse and the rec coordinator. And there's a psychologist and a psychiatrist. Half the time, I don't even know who they all are. And they've got reports on you and they read them out. I'm supposed to give my report on me, too, just so's I can feel included. So they all listen to my report, and then they tell me what's going to happen to me."

"But I don't want you to move to High Level."

"Me neither." He paused. "This weekend, I'm supposed to go for a visit. I think I move in two weeks. But they could dump me there this weekend. They've done it before."

"Oh." Sharon stared at the opposite wall.

"Things were finally starting to go okay."

"I don't want you to leave."

"I've got to go catch my bus." Richard reached out a hand to help her up.

"Isn't there anyone who'll listen to you?" she asked.

For the first time, Richard looked at her. "No."

That night, Sharon's room was a huge, black circle. Through the curtain, she could see the vague, white splotch of moon. She was in the middle of the Black Hole. It was like Richard's glass eye. Nothing moved.

Maybe that was what group homes did to you, she thought. Made it look like there was nothing you could do. Why didn't he want to try? He had to want to try. He *had* to.

Chapter 25

The next day, Richard wasn't out with the recess crowd, and they couldn't find him at lunch. Sharon and Fern scoured the grounds twice, then slipped back into the school and walked the halls. When they passed the office, they saw him slouched in a chair, ignoring some assigned work. Sharon could see the empty socket. He was keeping the glass eye in his pocket. Not a good sign.

He wasn't out for the afternoon break either. As soon as classes were over for the day, Sharon told Fern not to wait for her and ran down the hallway toward Mr. Ludlow's classroom. Through the open doorway, she could see a few kids. Richard was sitting at his desk, so she leaned against the wall a short way down the hall and waited. The other kids left, glancing at her as they passed.

"You waiting for Richard?" one of the girls asked.

"Yeah."

"He's got another detention. Been freaking out all day. Mouthing off, tearing up his work. Ludlow's really pissed off."

Mr. Ludlow closed the class door without noticing her. Sharon moved closer. The teacher's voice began in low tones. It went on and on. She imagined him stand-ing like Uncle Bert, legs spread apart, arms crossed, mouth moving and moving. When they got like this, they turned into some kind of robot. His voice became faster and louder. Any more and she'd be able to make out the words. Mr. Ludlow seemed to be repeating something over and over. Sharon pressed her ear against the door. Richard's voice came at last, low and gruff.

"What'd you say?" She could hear Mr. Ludlow's words now. "What'd you say, savage?"

She couldn't make out Richard's reply.

"What'd you say to me, savage?"

Someone started shoving desks. The voices talked fast, mixing together. Sharon stood on tiptoe and looked through the door window. She could see Richard by his desk, face tight and thin, fists clenched. He bent forward and screamed, "I don't have to take this! I'm getting out of here!" He lurched toward the door.

Mr. Ludlow stepped forward so that he blocked Sharon's view. Another desk moved as Richard tried to get to the door. Then Mr. Ludlow grabbed the back of Richard's jacket. Richard was trying to move away and the teacher was jerking him back around, half-lifting him off his feet.

Pressed against the classroom door, Sharon's weight pushed it open. She stumbled forward, tripping over her own feet. There was so much noise, no one noticed her. Mr. Ludlow had shoved Richard backward over a desk and was holding his shoulders down with both hands.

"Nuthin' but a savage, boy. You'll never be nuthin' but a savage," he said.

Richard stared up at Mr. Ludlow, his mouth trem-bling. "Go to hell."

Mr. Ludlow smiled and began to pull Richard to his feet. That was when he saw Sharon. The teacher froze, then jerked his hands off Richard. He seemed confused and took a step toward her.

"What're you doing in my classroom!" he demanded.

Sharon stared. "I was waiting for Richard."

"You should be waiting outside. Who gave you permission to enter?"

"No one, sir."

Behind the teacher, Sharon could see Richard quickly bend down, pull up his sweat pant leg and slide the panel on his false limb, releasing the vacuum.

"Leave this classroom immediately," snapped the teacher. He started to turn back to Richard.

Richard almost had it.

"Sir?" Sharon asked.

"What?" Mr. Ludlow turned back toward Sharon.

Now the sweat pant leg hung empty, shriveled up. Richard straightened, the false leg in his hand. As he leaned against a desk for balance, the desk shifted, scraping the floor. Quickly, Mr. Ludlow turned toward him and Richard swung the leg at him like a bat. It caught the teacher on the shoulder, then glanced up and off the side of his head. Richard fell back onto the desk. Mr. Ludlow staggered, swearing. There was a red spot forming on his forehead. Without a word, the teacher turned and walked out the door.

Breathing hard, Richard bent down and began to reattach his leg. "You're in trouble now," he said, not looking at her. "That's no good."

It was as if he'd left his own face and become another person—someone who didn't want her there. Sharon melted into a desk. "What about you?"

"I'm gone. Next week, I'll be someone else in High Level."

Mr. Ludlow walked back into the classroom followed by Mr. Sidlowski. The principal stood for a moment, looking from Sharon to Richard. Then he said, "Okay, let's get to the bottom of this. Richard, sit down."

Richard pulled down his sweat pant leg and sat down two seats over from Sharon without looking at her. She tried to swallow the loneliness that swam in her throat.

"Mr. Ludlow, why don't you explain what happened?" Mr. Sidlowski asked.

Mr. Ludlow's voice came out smooth, calm, and very quiet. "Last night, Richard got the news that he'd be moving soon to High Level and it has upset him. As you know, Mr. Sidlowski, this is often the case when one of our students from the Youth Center gets news of a move. Richard has been acting out all day. I kept him in after school to complete the work he refused to do this afternoon. He took off that peg leg and hit me on the head with it."

Mr. Sidlowski's face sagged. "I see," he murmured.

Richard stared at the floor.

"And how does Sharon Frejer come into this?" the principal asked.

"She came bursting in. I can see she might've misunderstood what was going on."

"I see," repeated Mr. Sidlowski. "If she's not really involved, would it be all right with you if I asked her to leave?"

"Certainly," agreed Mr. Ludlow.

Panic flickered through Sharon. Mr. Sidlowski was going to kick her out and listen to a lie. "No," she said quickly. "That's not what happened. I saw it."

Mr. Sidlowski blinked quickly. Mr. Ludlow's smile tightened. Richard stared out the window.

"As I said, I can see how you might've misunderstood," Mr. Ludlow repeated. His face looked concerned and fatherly—too fatherly. He wasn't her father. No one was her father. Sharon looked at Mr. Sidlowski. "I heard Mr. Ludlow yelling. He was calling Richard a savage. He called him that lots of times."

Mr. Ludlow cleared his throat. "I was referring to his savage behavior. I intended it to be interpreted in the dictionary meaning."

Fern's voice floated into Sharon's head. "Underline the subject with one red line. Underline the verb with two green lines. Underline the object with a wavy black line."

"You started everything," Sharon said. "You used savage as a noun, not an adjective. And you were shoving the desks first, and then you were shoving Richard."

"And then?" prompted Mr. Sidlowski.

"Well . . . then Richard pulled off his leg and hit Mr. Ludlow. But it was to keep him away. Mr. Ludlow was hurting him."

"I see," said Mr. Sidlowski. "Is there anything else you wanted to add?"

Her head turned toward Richard. She hesitated. He's my best friend, she wanted to say. He changed my whole life.

Finally, Richard looked at her. The thin, hard lines of his face stared back at her, so still, he seemed hardly alive.

"Thanks," he said.

Footsteps came quickly down the hall, and then a man stood in the classroom door. "I'm from the Youth Center," he said.

Mr. Sidlowski and Mr. Ludlow looked at each other in relief and stood up.

"How are you, Richard?" asked the man at the door.

That door would take him away. Richard would walk through it and never come back. Sharon stood up, walked over to Richard and took his hand. He didn't look at her, but his fingers tightened around hers. They walked, holding hands, down the long, empty hallway, through the push-handle doors, into the cold winter wind. At the far end of the parking lot, she could see a van parked. Again, Richard's hand tightened around hers.

Sharon's tears started. Mr. Sidlowski put a hand on her arm, gently pulling her away. A gust of wind came, lifting Richard's hair. She saw the man from the Youth Center put his arm around Richard, watched his one live eye turn toward her, reaching, like a hand. She knew then that this was what he'd expected all along.

Sharon strained against the principal's hand. Strange whimpers were coming from her throat. Now Richard had passed the two cars in the parking lot and was halfway to the van. Every second he looked smaller, farther away. Then he reached up and took the glass eye from its socket. His arm swung back and the eye was flying through the air, out across the parking lot and on into the copse among the bare-branched trees.

Chapter 26

Uncle Bert was at his curling club and her mother was watching TV. Sharon slipped down the backstairs wearing her orange jacket. Quiet as anything, she closed the back door. It was minus twenty out, but there was no wind. That'd help.

Behind the house was a small parking lot for Uncle Bert's two cars. Sharon set down the small, metal garbage pail she'd brought from her room. Then she opened the envelope containing the paper dolls with the blackened faces and watched them drift down into the pail. From a shoe box, she lifted out the rest of the paper dolls in clumps and dropped them. Then she stood, staring down into the pail.

In the dim light coming from the kitchen window, she could hardly make out the shapes jumbled around at the bottom of the pail. The last time she'd played with paper dolls had been during the Christmas holidays. That was almost two months ago.

"Let's burn them." Fern's voice blew through her mind and was gone. Sharon remembered the way she'd wanted to clutch the envelope of paper dolls to her chest. She wasn't that person anymore. It seemed years since she'd left Rockwood, since Fern had befriended her, since she'd started going out with Richard Calliou. *Going out* didn't seem to mean kissing or even holding hands much. What it meant was that when you walked into a crowded cafeteria, there was a face there waiting for you, wanting to spend time with you. Wanted. For the first time in her life, Sharon felt wanted.

Before supper, she'd tried to call the Youth Center, but she was told that Richard had lost his phone privileges. No one knew when he'd get them back.

Sharon stared down at the pail. Burning the paper dolls would mean the end of something, the end of a place inside of herself, a place she could never again go back to. It was the place inside the paper doll game where everything shut down and nothing moved. It was a place she didn't have to think. From now on, she was going to think. She was going to think all the time.

Reaching into her pocket, she pulled out a box of matches. She crouched down and struck one alight inside the pail. At the edge of the paper figures, the white-orange light flared up, then died down. It began to spread along the legs and arms, faces and long, flowing hair.

Sharon felt anger move through her in the same rhythm—a low, quiet flickering in her arms, chest, along her mouth. Anger. She knew what the feeling was now. All her life, she'd been feeling it deep inside herself, but she hadn't known what it was until now. Angry—she was angry.

When she could sift through the cooled ashes with her hand, Sharon poured them into the shoe box and closed the lid. Then she slipped back into the house, up the stairs, and placed the shoe box at the back of her closet in the darkest corner.

Chapter 27

"You think they'd let him back?" Fern asked. "After that fight with Ludlow?"

It was early the next morning and they were sitting on Fern's living room couch. Her parents had left for work. Her brother had an early morning band practice. Fern sat hunched, chin on knees. Sharon doodled on the cover of her science duotang. *STAY,* she wrote. *LET RICHARD STAY.* Her pen dug into the duotang cover, ripping the surface.

"They've got to listen," she said. "How do we make them listen?" Her pen tore deeper into the duotang cover. *LISTEN,* she wrote.

"Wait a minute!" Fern yelped. "We could make signs, like when people go on strike and march around yelling things."

"But we're not on strike," Sharon said.

"Yeah, I know," Fern said pointedly. "The signs and the yelling are to get attention, right? We write stuff on the signs about Richard staying, and we march around the school yelling." She demonstrated. "THIS IS A COVER-UP!" she yelled.

Sharon stared at her friend. *Marching. Yelling.*

Excited, Fern nodded. "They'll have to pay attention to us then. Especially if we march in front of that office."

The office. The place where Mr. Sidlowski pretended nothing was happening.

"Yeah," Sharon said. "The office. Let's march around the office. At lunch hour. Lots of people walk in and out of there then."

"We still have our lawn signs from the last election," Fern said. "Dad ran for city council. He lost, but he keeps his loser signs in the basement. We'll make our own signs and stick them over the old ones. We've got Bristol board."

Fern took off for the supplies. Sharon looked at the clock. 8:25 A.M. They had to move quickly. Once Richard was gone, it'd be impossible to get him back. If they could convince the school that Mr. Ludlow was the problem, then maybe the school would ask the Youth Center to send Richard back for his last two weeks in Edmonton.

Fern returned, waving two election signs.

"You think this'll do any good?" Sharon asked.

"It better," Fern said.

"Yeah," Sharon agreed. She sat with the Bristol board on her lap and thought. Fern's living room seemed to disappear. Her hand picked up the marker and wrote across the Bristol board.

"What's it say?" Fern leaned over her.

Sharon stared at her uneven printing. *LISTEN TO RICHARD. LET HIM DECIDE HIS LIFE.*

Fern nodded. Then she wrote: *MR. LUDLOW ASSAULTED RICHARD. THIS IS A COVER-UP.*

The two girls looked at each other. The whole thing seemed enormous. "Let's go," Fern said.

At lunchtime, they pulled their signs out of their

lockers and headed for the office. As the WELCOME TO THE OFFICE notice came into view, Sharon ducked in behind her hair. It had been a long morning and her stomach had clocked all of it. She could see teachers and students going in and out of the office doorway. The halls were full of kids headed for the cafeteria, intramurals, the library.

"Remember what we're supposed to say?" Fern asked.

Sharon nodded. They pulled garbage bags off their signs and pushed them into the air. Sharon fixed her eyes on the back of Fern's head and followed her around the front lobby.

"Let Richard stay!" Fern began to chant.

I can't do it, Sharon thought. Her voice was a weak echo. "Let Richard stay," she whispered.

Ahead of them, kids were staring, stepping aside to let them pass. Sharon kept her eyes on Fern, but she could see more and more feet turning and standing still.

"Mr. Ludlow attacked Richard Calliou!" Fern yelled. "This is a cover-up! Cover-up! Let Richard stay!"

Richard Calliou. Richard Calliou. Suddenly, Sharon could see his hand tossing the glass eye back and forth. *Richard.* The pang that shot through her hurt. And it was angry. *Angry.* Sharon realized she was angry. *Not afraid— angry.*

"Let Richard stay," she said more loudly. She shot a glance at the kids standing around. More were coming down the hall. Some teachers going into the office had turned to watch. Sharon pushed her sign higher.

"This is a cover-up," she chanted with Fern.

Off to one side, Frank gave them the thumbs-up sign.

"Get a sign and join us, Frank," Fern called.

Frank lost his grin and ducked into the library. They

kept going around the lobby, chanting, "Let Richard stay. Cover-up. Cover-up."

Ms. Okashimo was watching, a hand over her mouth. There were some new kids now—kids from Richard's class. She could see the two boys who'd yelled racist comments during the volleyball game. One of them pointed and laughed. Other kids joined in. The two boys turned and walked away, followed by a growing group.

No, thought Sharon. Stay and listen. *Listen*.

More and more kids were drifting away. They floated off down the hall in small groups. As they walked away, they seemed to take Sharon's voice with them. It grew softer and softer. No one was listening. No one cared.

Ahead of her, Fern's voice was doing the opposite. Fern was getting hoarse, but she yelled louder to make up for it.

Mr. Sidlowski walked in the school's front door and stopped dead in his tracks.

"Cover-up!" Fern yelled.

The principal's face filled with disgust. "This is enough!" he snapped, his hand reaching for Sharon's sign.

Sharon watched him grab it out of her hand. She knew it was her sign and her hand, but everything was going strange now. Her hand felt like it belonged to someone else, like it was a stranger's hand and no longer had anything to do with her. She was floating up and away from it.

At the same time, she turned toward Fern. She was trying to say, "Help me, it's going weird, it's going to happen again."

The Black Hole started to open up in her head. Sharon could feel the dizzy circle begin to spread out. But then the thought came back to her again: *Angry. Not afraid—ANGRY!*

The Black Hole closed up. Sharon turned and grabbed at her sign.

"It's my sign!" Sharon shouted.

Mr. Sidlowski let go.

"Cover-up!" Sharon yelled.

"Into my office now," Mr. Sidlowski said. "Fern—that includes you."

"Yes, sir," said Fern, staring at Sharon.

"And bring those signs," the principal ordered. "Now."

Chapter 28

"Sharon, Sharon, Sharon," her mother said. "I can't believe you did this."

It was late that afternoon. Sharon sat on her bed, staring at her feet. Her mother sat on a wooden chair, staring at her. She had dark shadows under her eyes and kept twisting her watch around her wrist. "I don't know what your Uncle Bert is going to do about this," she muttered.

Sharon had been in Mr. Sidlowski's office when the principal phoned Uncle Bert at his store. She'd heard the long silence at the other end of the phone when the principal had said Sharon and Fern were to be suspended for two days. She'd been afraid then, and she was afraid now. Fear was like water filling up her legs and stomach. It had waves like an ocean in a storm.

"I'm sorry," Sharon said. "I didn't mean to upset you."

Fern had been driven home by her mother. Sharon had walked home alone through the winter-gray afternoon. All the way, she'd counted things—sidewalk cracks, hydro poles.

"I wish . . ." started her mother, then stopped.

"You wish what?" Sharon asked dully.

"That you were happy," her mother said, looking out the window. She ran a hand over her face. "What do I do about this? Your uncle is so angry."

The question walked out of Sharon's mouth. "Mom? What're you so afraid of?"

Her mother stopped moving and closed her eyes.

"Please tell me what it is," Sharon said.

Her mother sat so still. Sharon put out a hand and touched her arm.

"All we wanted was for someone to listen," Sharon said. "How come people can just do that to Richard? How come he can't stay when that's what he wants?" She brushed the tear-wet hair out of her face. "Fern and Richard—they're the first friends I've ever had. My *first* friends."

Her mother winced and closed her eyes. "I know, honey," she said.

Sharon stopped trying to stop crying. "Why can't you get a job? So we can live on our own?"

"I have a job. I work in the store."

"A different job," Sharon said. "Away from him. Can't you go to school at night?"

"There's the bookkeeping. I have to clean the house. I have to cook supper. I have to do the dishes."

"I'll do it," Sharon said. "I'll help you."

"You have your homework." Her mother's eyes were staring at things Sharon couldn't see. "I want you to be different from me, little girl," she said. "I want your life to be different than mine. My parents . . . they always told your Uncle Bert and Uncle Lawrence and me that we couldn't do anything. We were no good. Stupid. Your uncles got beat up every day."

Sharon stopped breathing. "What happened to you?"

"Someday I'll tell you," her mother said softly. "You're too young now."

Sharon could see her uncles' faces in her head. They were little boys and they were crying. Then she saw them grown up and watching TV. They looked half dead.

"I guess we believed what we were told," her mother said slowly. "When they tell you it enough, you believe them."

"It wasn't true," Sharon said.

"No, it wasn't." Her mother glanced at her. "And you know, I'm starting to see that. I'm thirty-two years old, and I'm finally starting to see that."

"You can do it, Mom. Whatever you want."

Sharon's mother gave a shaky smile and touched her daughter's face. "So you think I should go back to school, eh?"

"Yeah."

"I want to."

"I'll do the dishes. Honest."

"Honey, you'd scrape dirt off the ceiling for me." Sharon's mother stood up and walked to the door. "I'm sorry you lost your friend. I'll talk to your Uncle Bert again."

Her mother seemed different, as if something new was happening inside. She took a deep breath, looked at Sharon and their eyes met.

"And you think of a way to explain this to him, too," she said grimly.

Chapter 29

When she woke up, it was evening. Downstairs, there were voices arguing. Her mother's came in short bursts. Uncle Bert's rose around hers, a rough, dark sound. There was some banging and Sharon guessed a fist was pounding the kitchen table. Her mother fell silent. A chair squeaked as it was pushed back. The door at the bottom of the stairs opened. Sharon tensed.

"No, Bert." It was her mother. "She's my daughter. I'll deal with it. I promise you she won't do it again."

The door closed and the voices continued more quietly. Sharon got up and tiptoed down the long, cold hall. She ran the water slowly so the pipes wouldn't make much noise. Her reflection in the mirror looked red and puffy. Her bedspread pattern was pressed into one cheek.

Sharon stared at the eyes, nose, mouth, then back to the eyes. Brown eyes, with flecks of blue and hazel stared back. There was no one new there—just the same old Sharon Frejer she'd always been. And downstairs was the same old Uncle Bert.

He heard her on the stairs. The sofa springs squeaked as Uncle Bert jumped up and strode into the kitchen. He was waiting when she slid through the door.

"Bert!" Her mother came out of the pantry.

He ignored her. "What the hell d'you think you were trying to pull?" he roared. "What kind of stoopid idiot do I have living under my roof?"

Sharon fought with her chin, pushing it up.

"Bert," her mother repeated.

"What a stoopid thing to do. You're a bloody idiot—d'you know that?"

Steady as an elevator now, Sharon's eyes were moving up from the floor, up along the gray pants he wore in the store, the beige shirt with the small, brown ducks, the lined throat, up to the face with the heavy, dark eyes, brown-black, like Uncle Lawrence's. In the middle of the white kitchen his eyes hung, glaring at her. It seemed to her that they'd been there all her life in her head, watching everything she said or did, what she thought.

"Stoopid!" Uncle Bert waved his finger at her.

Sharon saw Uncle Lawrence's face flash across Uncle Bert's so that both were there together.

"Spirit-eater," Richard said.

"Die denken sind frei," Fern's voice whispered to her.

"Stoopid," Uncle Bert muttered again, his hand dropping.

A long way down in her gut, so far down it seemed to be forever on its way, anger was coming to Sharon—anger that had always been there, anger that needed out. It grew until it was everywhere in her. It was everything she needed. It was as huge as sky.

"No," she said loudly. She pushed back some hair that'd fallen into her eyes and stared straight into his face.

"I'm not convinced," Sharon said. "I'm not convinced I'm stupid."

Uncle Bert took a step toward her, his hand rising.

"No—Bert!" her mother cried, moving in behind him.

Inside Sharon, the hugeness collapsed. She turned and ran up the stairs, slammed her door and leaned against it, looking for something to drag across it.

But there were no footsteps following, heavy on the stairs, no fist pounding on the door. Slowly, Sharon stopped shaking. Downstairs, she heard her mother's voice, then the creaking sound as Uncle Bert sat down heavily on the sofa and lost himself in the light of the TV.

Chapter 30

It was Color Night. Sharon stood next to Fern, wearing a yellow shirt and a gold armband. That afternoon, their class had painted Gold Team banners in L.A. Now the school was gathered in the gym, a mass of gold, green, red, and blue shirts, each team screaming its cheer at full volume.

Sharon couldn't get into it. She'd promised to be here because of Richard. Every time she turned around, part of her expected to see him come around a corner. She stood in the middle of the crowd, plugging her ears and waiting for the cheers to end.

The suspension from school had been several weeks back. Since then, things at school had changed. Everyone treated her differently. Ms. Okashimo kept smiling at her and calling on her in class. Mr. Sidlowski always looked annoyed and very busy whenever he saw her. Mr. Ludlow walked the other way. Ms. Bohn left her alone, and Sharon finally tried out a sewing machine. It didn't blow up and she passed her pot-holder project.

Most of the kids had stopped making paper doll jokes. She'd made a few more friends. Everything had become so different that she could sometimes forget the strange heaviness that pressed down around her. For hours, she'd forget why, then suddenly remember. Richard was gone now. The heaviness Sharon felt was his gone-ness.

Tonight, she was in the bean bag throw. That was the event she'd chosen when Richard's Finger of Doom had gone down the list that February afternoon. "You've got to pick something," he'd insisted. She'd figured then that the bean bag event would get little attention. She was right. It took place in the Home Ec. room. The only kids present were the four participants and Fern, who cheered and jumped up and down in her rubber boots. Sharon rolled her eyes, but she did look when she threw the bean bags. The Gold Team came in second.

"Richard would be impressed," said Fern.

Sharon stood against the stage, watching Fern play volleyball. Even in rubber boots, Fern was able to jump above the net and smash the ball down onto the other side. Once the volleyball bounced off of her face, but she laughed, giving herself the crazy sign with her index finger.

Sharon didn't watch the end of the game. She walked away in search of a place where no one was running or screaming. They'd all forgotten Richard so fast. It was as if he'd never been here, never paid attention to her, never helped her look for her retainer. Changed her life. At the end of a hallway, she leaned against the concrete wall, feeling her face go hot. Here, at last, it was quiet.

The distant noise from the gym faded. Color Night was almost over. Someone had a megaphone and was announcing an event. Suddenly, Sharon realized it was the race around the gym—Richard's race. But he wouldn't be there. Anger whirled through her. She turned and ran for the gym. Someone had to be there for him.

Kids crowded the doors, but Sharon shoved through into the gym. There was a brief, clear silence, then the clash of cymbals. A cheer went up as four kids pushed themselves up from the starting line. There was a girl in a blue shirt—Richard's replacement.

"Where'd you go?" Fern asked, leaning against her.

Sharon shrugged. The runners were one quarter of the way around now, their faces twisted with the effort. That was when she saw Richard step from the crowd and kneel at the starting line. As if he'd been waiting for her, he looked straight at her, grinned, and ducked his head.

He was only there in her head. She knew this.

Once again, Sharon heard the cymbals clash. She knew this was only in her head, too. Then the Richard whom only she saw pulled himself up and stepped forward onto his false leg. His thin body lunged down, sloping into the step, then rose into the movement of the good leg. The others were now halfway around the gym, and he was far behind, but it didn't seem to matter. He kept coming around the track, body rising and falling like a wave, every bone and muscle pushing him forward. She saw how his hands pumped him on, the way his mouth reached and gasped for air. His face wore the empty eye socket like a medallion, and the live eye shone.

The others had crossed the finish line and the Red Team was screaming victory. Beside her, Fern yelled something. Sharon ignored her. Richard was still coming around the track, halfway now, and inside, her heart was like a bird pushing upward, discovering flight.

For tonight, she knew why. She knew why he'd signed up for this race. It was in the running. The race was there for the running. It had nothing to do with crossing the finish line first.

He was three quarters around now. This was her race, too, Sharon thought. This was everyone's race. No one who ran it could be called "stoopid," "savage," or "not good enough."

Kids were walking across the gym, not feeling Richard pass through them. Sharon watched his back weave its way through the crowd and close in on the EXIT sign at the far side. He had come back to show her this, and now he was leaving again.

She smiled and watched him fade out. He would be back again. If she knew anything, she knew that once someone came to live inside her head, he came back time and time again. Richard would always be there.

Chapter 31

The spring wind blew roughly around the school. Small patches of snow lay, dirty white, on the muddy ground. Fern's boots squelched as she walked. It was spring break and the two of them were circling the school, peering into the darkened windows.

"It's like a tomb in there," Fern said.

Sharon was holding the shoe box of paper doll ashes to her chest. The box was so light, it could've been filled with nothing. That was what Uncle Lawrence was starting to feel like these days. She could see now that Uncle Lawrence wasn't everywhere. Knowing this helped her relax in Uncle Bert's house. She walked up and down the stairs without tiptoeing. When she lay in bed at night, she let go of her muscles one by one and let them go soft. She stopped thinking so hard all the time, and her brain seemed to enjoy that quite a bit. But she stayed careful around Uncle Bert. It was still *his* house, and he still yelled at the news, especially when land claims issues came up.

Still, he *was* helping her mother with her homework. Two nights a week, Sharon's mother was attending classes to finish her high school diploma. Uncle Bert was good at math, and he really got into it. He'd hunch over the kitchen table and jab at this or that with his finger, explaining things with his face just inches from Sharon's mother's face. It was sort of like having a bull dog for your tutor, Sharon thought, but her mother did seem to catch on to things more quickly with his explanations. Maybe Uncle Bert would actually help her mother get a job and a house of her own. Uncle Bert! People were confusing like that.

In the school parking lot, Fern was looking at the empty flagpole. Sharon could tell her friend was thinking about climbing it and flying herself like the Canadian flag.

"No pole climbing. We've got a job to do here," she said.

"All right, all right, Lieutenant Frejer," Fern replied. "Where d'you want to do this?"

"Over there." Sharon pointed to the edge of the parking lot, close to the copse of poplar trees where they'd had their first conversation with Richard. They'd looked for his glass eye in there several times, but it was gone. Someone else must have taken it.

She'd gotten a letter from him last week—her first. He'd written to her at the school address. "Sharon Frejer, please report to the office," had come over the PA. She'd stood up and walked through everyone's stares, wondering if she was about to be suspended again. This time, however, the secretary smiled at her and handed her a sealed envelope. *R. Calliou* was written in the top left corner.

"From a friend?" the secretary asked.

"Yes!" Sharon had darted out of the office and torn the envelope open in the empty hall. *Dear Sharon.* She'd read those two words over ten times before she went on to the next part. He said he'd moved in with his brother,

Matt, and was going to a new school in High Level. He was supposed to have been living in a group home, but Ms. Okashimo had called his social worker. They'd had a long talk.

It's okay living with Matt, Richard wrote. *It's home. You know it when you find it.*

Standing in the school yard, holding the shoe box, Sharon felt his letter resting in her pocket, something warm and wanted.

When you and Fern stuck up for me in Sid's office, at first I had to laugh at it, Richard had said. *No one ever did that for me before. I thought it was some kind of new game, especially for Fern. She's not bad, once you get used to her.*

I think about you. How you talked back to Sid and Ludlow together. I wonder if even Fern could do that. You're a good friend, Sharon Frejer. You got what it takes.

Send me a picture, okay?

He'd signed his name next to an *X*. Sharon flushed, thinking about it. A picture. She'd have to wear barrettes for that.

A gust of wind whipped by and back again. "We have to wait until the wind blows toward the north," she said. "High Level is north."

Solemnly, Fern reached into a pocket and pulled out a piece of paper folded many times. She opened it and cleared her throat. "A Poem For Richard Calliou," she read.

Friends tie an invisible string
that runs from one heart
to another heart to another
and so on around the world.
It goes everywhere they go.
This string is made up of everything
they said and did together.

It keeps them always friends.
Sometimes you can't see a friend.
You wonder where he is,
what he's doing.
You miss him.
Then you remember the string
and you pull on it.
He's there again.

Sharon listened, a new smile on her mouth. As she turned to face north, the wind came running toward her, lifting back her hair, pouring over her forehead, nose, cheeks. She felt it touch her mouth, slide over her chin. It was there, her face—complete, solid, something she could live within.

"You should've written a poem, too," Fern said. Suddenly, her face screwed itself up. "I think this is it!" She licked her finger and held it up. "Quick, Frejer—it's headed north!"

Sharon flung the lid off the shoe box. Inside, small swirls of ash began to lift. With a quick glance at Fern, she said, "This is a poem."

It was her good-bye to the Black Hole. Sharon's body came together in a giant, swinging motion that sent the paper doll ashes up and out. For a moment, they hung together, a sort of gray-black place, midair against the swaying trees. Then the wind sucked them up, and the ashes scattered, dissolved into the thin blue of the great north sky.

R. Ross Annett Award
for Children's Literature

Canadian Children's
Book Centre Our
Choice Award

Governor General's
Award nomination for
Children's Literature

Also by Beth Goobie:

Mission Impossible

Jill doesn't like the high school Lovely Legs Competition. For one thing, it's sponsored by the football team headed by her brother. For another, the school newspaper she writes for came up with the idea. But more important, it boils her blood that guys like her brother make so many assumptions about what girls like. So why does she end up entering the competition? Maybe for the same reason she tried out for the football team. Maybe for the same reason she's obsessed with the movie *The Mission*. Jill comes close to going over the edge in more ways than one but triumphs in a way she could never have predicted.

"[Goobie] demonstrates talent and understanding; above all, she creates a voice that speaks to modern teens." –Starred Review, Quill & Quire

"Zippy pace and an insightful rendering of adolescence in the 1990s." –Globe and Mail

"Articulates the feelings and fears of young women in a way that even the most macho football captain would find difficult to ignore. . . . Seriously good." –Calgary Herald